"THE FINEST OF ALL SCOTLAND YARD
SERIES."
— *The New York Times*

A figure appeared in front of her, the figure of a
leaping man.

Before she could scream, the man's hands were at her
throat. She felt the pressure of his fingers, suddenly and
savagely brutal.

She couldn't breathe, had no hope at all of shouting,
of calling for help. His face was close to hers, a hideous,
grinning face, a *mask* of a face.

Then she saw the knife, bright and glinting in his
other hand.

"THE GIDEON NOVELS WILL UNDOUBTEDLY
BECOME TWENTIETH-CENTURY CLASSICS."
— *The Providence Sunday Journal*

"EXCELLENT MYSTERY SUSPENSE."
Erle Stanley Gardner

"COMMANDER GEORGE GIDEON OF
SCOTLAND YARD CAN ALWAYS BE
COUNTED ON FOR AN EVENING OF
SURPRISINGLY EXCITING COMPANIONSHIP."

— *The Washington Star*

EDGAR AWARD WINNER
J·J· MARRIC
Gideon's Night

ZEBRA BOOKS
KENSINGTON PUBLISHING CORP.

ZEBRA BOOKS

are published by

Kensington Publishing Corp.
475 Park Avenue South
New York, NY 10016

First Zebra Books printing: August, 1989

Printed in the United States of America

1

Night's Beginning

In the early, misty dusk, Gideon stepped out of his
house and closed the door on brightness and music. It
was not yet six o'clock. His family, except Matthew,
who was out, would spend the evening gathered round
the fire, the television, lesson books and, if Prudence
could make the others sit back for half an hour, her
violin. It was a happy family, happier today than it had
been a few years ago, when he and Kate had drawn
apart; and he was thinking about that. For when he had
kissed Kate good-by she had held him tightly for a
moment, not wanting him to go out into London's
night. At one time she simply had not cared and neither
had he. Now they were man and wife if ever two people
were—and at this moment Kate was back in the living
room, exerting her firm but often unsuspected control
over the family.

It was chilly.

Gideon shrugged his big body inside the thick gray
overcoat, a massive man with slightly rounded
shoulders, a fine head, rather heavy features. He had a
slow, deliberate walk, because he had trained himself

5

not to hurry except in emergency, and he was in good time. On the nights which he was going to spend in his office at the Yard, or out and about on the Yard's business, he liked to arrive fairly early. Lemaitre and other daytime-duty men would wait to brief him with the day's happenings, and he did not want to keep them too late.

He walked toward his garage, round the corner.

This was Hurlingham, part of the London suburb of Fulham, where he had lived most of his life and all of his marriage, yet the night scene had freshness: the haloes round the street lamps, the lights at windows where neighbors lived with their troubles and their problems—and where, only a few weeks ago, a regular patron of the magistrates' courts had broken in, by night, and got away with three hundred pounds' worth of jewelry.

Gideon, Commander George Gideon of the Criminal Investigation Department of the Metropolitan Police, hadn't yet lived that down. He smiled dryly at the thought now. The thief was in jail, most of the jewelry had been recovered, and the men at the Yard had had their little joke.

He reached the corner.

A tall man was just along the street, beyond the garage, and looked as if he had been lounging against the wall and had just straightened up. Suspiciously? The thought was hardly in Gideon's mind when he recognized the "man" and his smile turned into a grin. This was Matthew, his seventeen-year-old son, thin and spindly although possessed of broad shoulders and big hips; he would fill out, but at the moment could hardly be more awkward or cumbersome. He was the ugly duckling, anyhow, with plain features and invariably untidy hair, but the greatest cause for worry was about his future. He was clever, almost brilliant in his studies, but had always been vague about what he wanted to do. He seemed to think that the world would fall into his lap.

Obviously he had been waiting here, so he had something to say to his father that he didn't want to say in front of his mother.

"Hello, Matt, just coming home?"

"Evening, Dad. Yes, I—I was kept in this afternoon. I'm a bit late."

"Feel sorry for you young hopefuls sometimes," said Gideon, in a tone which obviously had Matthew guessing; was this sincere or was it parental sarcasm? "In my young days school finished about four o'clock, and we had an hour's homework to do, if we had the sense to do it." Gideon was unlocking the big green doors of the garage, and Matthew stood ready to push the sliding doors to one side.

"I know," he said quietly and hurriedly. "I'm just about fed up with school. They don't really teach you anything worth while. What the dickens is the use of learning about algebraic problems and logarithms and Greek gods? Why, there are times when—"

He pushed the door and it ran easily on the runners; a sharp noise as it banged against the stop cut off his last words.

"I mean, do you know anything about Greek gods?" he demanded hotly.

"Not much," conceded Gideon. "It takes me all my time to sort out what's true of one." He was troubled, because he was coming to the opinion that Matthew simply didn't like work, and, if Gideon had a hate, it was of laziness. But nothing of this sounded in his voice as he went on: "Lend a hand with the car, will you?"

There was no room to open the door and get to the wheel while the car was in the garage, which was too narrow for it to be backed inside with any safety. So it

7

had to be pulled by the bumper until the door was clear. At one time that had been a nuisance but now it was almost second nature; garages weren't easy to come by in London.

They pulled.

"Dad, *must* I stay until I'm eighteen?" Matthew burst out. "Why can't I leave at the end of this term? There's no law to make me stay, fifteen's the legal leaving age, and even if I did win a scholarship to a university, what use is it to me? It isn't as if I wanted to be a professor or a mathematician or—or—"

"A student of Greek mythology," Gideon completed for him. "Nip in the other side, while I get the car off the pavement." He got into the Wolseley and switched on the ignition, while Matthew scrambled in the other side as eagerly as he had when he had been a child. Gideon started the engine and reversed slowly. He seldom talked while he was reversing, or driving in traffic, and Matthew knew better than to expect conversation. He pulled in to the curb. "When's your mother expecting you home?"

"Oh, I'm late, but she won't worry how much—"

"You'd be surprised how much she might worry," said Gideon. "You'd better pop in and tell her you're back and that you're coming with me for the drive."

"Oh, *fine!*" breathed Matthew.

Two minutes later, the front door closed on Penelope, the youngest girl, and Matthew came hurrying back. He slammed the car door, and settled down.

"Dad, I *thought* you'd understand. I'm tired of school. I want to get a job and start earning some money, instead of sponging on you all the time. Tom left school at fifteen and he's done well for himself, hasn't he? I know he's much older than I am but—well, he's actually going to get *married*. He must be earning a whopping big screw. If I don't start soon, what chances

8

have I got of succeeding?"

Tom, Gideon's oldest son, had lived away from home for several years.

"I see," said Gideon, as he drove at fair speed along the narrow street. "Know what you want to do for a living, Matt?"

"Yes!" The word came out almost defiantly. "I've decided."

"Hmm." Gideon managed to his surprise. Now that it had come, he wasn't sure that he liked the thought of Matthew with his mind made up in such a way that he didn't want to tell his mother; even defiant because he was sure that he would run into opposition.

"What's it to be?" Gideon made himself sound eager.

Matthew turned to stare at his father. As they passed a street lamp, Gideon took his eye off the road for a moment, so as to glimpse the eager face, the unusually bright eyes, one hand raised and clenched as a measure of the lad's intensity.

"I want to be a policeman, a copper. I want to start in the ranks and work my way up, just like you did!"

"Good God!" exclaimed Gideon.

"I know Mum won't like it. I don't suppose you will either. Mum's always complaining that she's never known where you'd be from one moment to the next— why, look at tonight. She hates it when you go out on night duty, and whenever you're called up in the middle of the night, well, you ought to hear what she *says* sometimes. I know she's frightened, but that—"

"Frightened?"

"Of course she is, especially since that time when you were looking for Sid Benson," Matthew rushed on. "She just can't stand it when she thinks you might be in danger, but that's just *like* a woman. Women simply can't understand that a man *has* to have some adventure. What would life be like if there wasn't any danger? And after all, you've lived to be pretty old, haven't you?"

Gideon slowed down at a junction with a main road.

"I'll give you old," he said roundly. "I'm fifty-one, my lad, and fifty-one's no age. So you really want to start as a copper, you think your mother will hate the idea, and that I'll tell you to stop talking nonsense. That right?"

"Well, yes, won't you?"

They turned into the main road. It was fairly well lit just here, and there was more traffic, but not enough to be troublesome. Matthew still looked as if nothing but this subject mattered even slightly. Two policemen stood at a corner, and one saluted as Gideon's car passed, while both of them watched.

"Well, *won't* you?" demanded Matthew.

"Do you know, Matt, I'm not quite sure," said Gideon. That was true. "I'm really not sure. In some ways I'd like to feel that one of my boys was coming into the Force. It can be a damned good career. You might be right about your mother, but if you want a thing like this badly enough you'll have to show her that it really matters to you; then, even if she doesn't like it, she won't be unreasonable. But you've a lot of time for thinking about it, Matt, and you've got a few ideas that won't do you much good if you want to be a copper. Unless that's *all* you want to be," he added dryly, "a chap pushing a bike around, with a possibility of becoming a sergeant if you'll wait fifteen years or so."

"Of course that's not what I want! I want to do detective work in the C.I.D., like you. After all, you're right at the top—"

"If you forget the Assistant Commissioner for Crime, that's right," agreed Gideon, smothering a grin. "But all you can see is where I am, not how I got there and what I learned on the way." He paused to negotiate three cyclists who were riding abreast, and then swept forward along a nearly empty road leading to the heart

10

of London. Traffic coming out was getting thick. "If you do want to study for the C.I.D., the more you can learn at school and even the university—"

"But Dad, what use are—"

"Greek gods, I know," said Gideon, and he wasn't smiling. "The answer is that they might make or break you—certainly they might make you. It's about seven years since they dug up that statue of Minerva out of the ruins of the Barbican. It had lain under the ground for about fifteen hundred years. Funny thing, coincidence, but about a year afterward a lot of Greek and Roman pottery was found in France, caused quite a stir in archaeological and historical quarters, and some of the stuff was extremely valuable. Soon afterward it was stolen. You should have heard the screams that went up. It so happened that we had a youngish chap at the Yard who'd been interested about the stuff they dug up at the Barbican, and had learned a lot about it. We had a pretty good idea that one of several wealthy collectors had stolen the new discovery, or bought it from the thief. Our chap was able to mix with the suspect collectors, talk their own language, and find the stuff. One of the collectors had bought it, knowing it to be stolen—the thief got five years and the receiver three. That chap's got a lot to thank his interest in Greek gods for, Matt. He's a Divisional detective inspector today. If it hadn't been for that job he would probably be a detective sergeant at the Yard running around and doing what I tell him."

Matthew made no immediate response, and Gideon drove more quickly. In less than ten minutes they would be at the Yard, and he was falling behind time. Yet he didn't want to cut Matthew short.

Then Matthew said abruptly, "I suppose you really mean that *anything* a man knows might come in useful in detective work."

"Not might, Matt. It's bound to, sooner, or later.

11

It won't always be spectacular, but you've got to be a jack-of-all-trades, as well as knowing the ropes and routine. Know what detection is, really? It's patience, persistence, a good memory and a first-class power of observation. You come across some little thing in a case; let's take something simple like a foreign language. I've often heard you saying that you hate French lessons. Well, any Yard man who can speak and read French fluently is a step ahead of another chap who's just as competent in all other ways. Why? Because every week, sometimes a dozen times a week, we pick up a Frenchman or we have to question a French witness, and it can save a hell of a lot of time and trouble if we can do without an official interpreter. The more you know, Matt, the more chance you've got of getting on. Like to know something else? I didn't know a word of French before I joined the Force, but when I realized how much it might help I spent most of my spare time picking it up. You ought to have heard what your mother said about my nose being stuck in a book!"

Matthew grinned.

"I can imagine," he said slyly. "I think I see what you mean, Dad. General knowledge is very important."

"General knowledge is *all* important," corrected Gideon, "and all the special training, the routine, the walking the beat and taking your turn at traffic duty won't help if you haven't got it. Supposing we had trouble with a musician, for instance—the things that Pru can tell me about music would be as much use as anything else I know."

Matthew nodded again and was silent, but that didn't mean that he was subdued. They reached Parliament Square, where the yellow face of Big Ben was shrouded in mist, and where the lights of Westminster Bridge were clearly visible at this end, but vague and misty at the middle and beyond.

"Well, think about it," said Gideon more briskly. "Don't be in too much of a hurry. If I were you I'd wait a few weeks and then have another talk with me. There's no point in worrying your mother if it's going to come to nothing, is there? Now I'll have to look slippy. Got your fare home?"

"I—well, I *am* a bit short," Matthew said, and grinned. "You couldn't send me home in a prowl car, could you?"

"I could not! We don't have prowl cars; we have Squad cars and patrol cars, and the drivers are too busy to be running infants about." Gideon turned into the courtyard of Scotland Yard, from the Embankment, and pulled up, stopped the engine, and then took two half crowns from his pocket. "Here you are, and get that nonsense about sponging on me out of your head. What do you think I work for? Lot of use money would be to me if I didn't have a family to spend it on."

"Thanks, Dad." Matthew took the five shillings thoughtfully, and they got out and met at the back of the car. A tall flight of stone steps led up in front of them, and the tall, pale building rose high above their heads. "It's going to be a nasty night," Matthew observed casually. "Isn't this the kind of night that the Prowler gets around?"

There was a hint of excitement in his voice, after all.

"It's just the Prowler's kind of night, but when you get home you tell your mother there's hardly a trace of fog," ordered Gideon. He looked up as a plain-clothes man approached from the Embankment, brisk, heavily built, footsteps very firm. "Hello, Joc," Gideon greeted. "How about finding time to take my son Matthew down to the Information Room and let him see how it works? He has an idea that a policeman's life is full of excitement."

Matthew caught his breath, gazing at the newcomer as if willing him to say yes.

13

"Dullest place in London, this is," said the plain-clothes man, "but I don't think it'll be dull everywhere tonight. It's just the fog the Prowler ordered. All right, Matthew."

"Oh, *thank* you, sir!"

"Pleasure."

"Should've introduced you," Gideon said. "Matt, this is Chief Detective Inspector Whittaker."

Whittaker offered his hand, Matthew took it eagerly, and Gideon smiled but was a little uneasy as he went with them to the big hall, and then left them for the lift and his own office, his desk, the reports from the day men, the early reports of the night's accidents. It was quite dark now, and a lot of bad men were on the prowl—

Prowl.

Words came in spasms, sometimes, like varieties of crime. Get one report of robbery with violence and three or four were likely to come within a few hours. Hear of one race-horse-doping job, and there'd be a crop of them. They seemed to go in cycles, like playing with conkers, bowling hoops, spinning tops, tossing the yoyo and the roller-skating. A week or so would pass without a smash-and-grab job, and there would be half a dozen on the same day. At the Yard, and particularly in his job, you accepted the inevitability of crime which never stopped; you could never really get on top of it.

But you could stop some aspects of it, and usually you could catch a particular man if you really went all out. That was why he had chosen tonight to come on duty. The morning weather forecast had been "smoke and fog in towns and industrial areas tonight, clearing toward morning," and he wanted to know a lot more than he did about the Prowler, who always spread his terror on a foggy night.

14

2

The First Reports

The Yard was strange and even a little eerie by night, especially if you didn't come after dark very often. Now it was at its worst: dead, flat, drab, almost dreary. Young Matt had dreams of romance and adventure and there could be a little of both; a needle of romance and a pin of adventure in a haystack of routine and crime. Never mind young Matt. The passages of the C.I.D. buildings were fairly wide, and the cement of the floor and the walls seemed new—and also harsh and cold. The whole place struck cold, if it came to that. Doors were closed, and none opened, no one came walking along briskly, full of the next task to be done. The administrative staff was out and away, at home, the pictures, the theater, clubs, with girl of boy friend, mistress or wife, so the Yard was empty but for one or two key people, except in the C.I.D. section.

A door opened, brighter light shone into the dingy light of the passage, and a stocky man appeared, bustling, a sheaf of papers in his hand. This was an Inspector from Records. He wore pince-nez

"Hello, George," he said. "You on tonight?"

"Yes, Syd, got to make sure I don't slip."

"You slipped as far as you ever will years ago," said Syd dryly. "Looks as if you've picked a good one." He fell into step as they walked toward Gideon's office. The Records man was half a head shorter than Gideon, going bald where Gideon had a lot of thick, wiry gray hair.

"What's on?"

"What isn't?" Syd asked. "Lemaitre will tell you. He's waiting, and—mind if I have a word in your ear?"

"Nothing's ever stopped you yet."

Syd grinned, but spoke seriously.

"Don't keep Lemaitre any longer than you can help tonight. He's having another basinful of wife trouble. And if you can keep your other ear open while I whisper in that, too, if you want to keep Lem from going crazy, persuade him to walk out on his Fifi. She gets worse and he gets—well, the truth is any man who marries the lush and sexy type ought not to be surprised if he runs into trouble."

They stopped outside Gideon's brown door, which had the word COMMANDER printed on it, in black. Gideon had his back to the door and looked down at the Chief Inspector of Records.

"Got any facts?"

"You've got eyes."

"Any real reason to think it's any worse than it was, Syd?" Gideon asked in a quiet but insistent tone.

"As a matter of fact, I have," said Syd. "I was out in KI Division this afternoon, where Lem lives. The boys know all about Fifi and her goings on, and of late she's had one or two boy friends who didn't kiss good night on the right side of the door. Lemaitre got home early one night and saw one of these gentry leaving. There was a mother and father of a row. One of the local coppers heard it. That was a week ago—all's been quiet

16

and peaceful since then, but if Fifi breaks out again—" Syd paused, and frowned. "Don't tell me that you hadn't noticed anything wrong with Lem. He isn't that good at fooling you."

"I knew there was something wrong," said Gideon, "but I couldn't get anything out of him. Thanks, Syd."

"Okay, Gee-Gee!"

The Records man went on, and Gideon opened the door of his office. It was like opening a door into a steam oven. The "steam" was cigarette smoke, which was thick and pale, and the heat came from radiators which had spasms of working as if made exclusively for the Arctic, and at other times were barely warm.

At one end of the long room with windows overlooking the Embankment, Chief Inspector Lemaitre sat back in a chair, halfway through a cigarette, and a sergeant stood by him, glancing around. The sergeant, dressed in thick brown serge and wearing a collar and tie, looked too hot even to breathe comfortably, and his face was bright red. Lemaitre's was pale, his eyes were a little glittery, he had his coat off, his waistcoat was unbuttoned, and the ends of his yellow-and-black tie hung from a collar which had been wrenched from its stud.

"Hello," said Gideon. "Sorry I'm late."

"Good evening, sir." That was the sergeant.

"S'all right," said Lemaitre gruffly. "It doesn't matter to me whether I get home tonight." That was an effort to be funny and it failed completely. "What's the fog like?"

"Nothing much, yet."

"Going to be just about right for the Prowler," Lemaitre remarked. "You take it from me, George, one of these days the Prowler's going to leave a corpse behind, not just a girl who's scared stiff and got a nasty memory. Seven times is too many times to get away

17

with it." He stood up as Gideon went to his larger desk which was at the other end of the room. Gideon took off his coat and draped it over the back of his chair, then took a pipe out of his pocket. It had a very large bowl, and was rough on the outside; knobbly, too. He began to fill it slowly from a brown leather pouch.

"Tell you another thing," Lemaitre went on, while the sergeant stood and waited for instructions. "You're going to have one hell of a night. Never known so much to come in between six and seven o'clock. Having a bit of a lull now, but that won't last for long. What do you want first, the day's stuff or what's doing at the moment?"

"We got any leads?"

"Not really."

"Give me the day's stuff, will you?" Gideon said. "Sergeant, pull up a chair and make notes when I tell you to."

"Yes, sir."

"Oh, bring up a chair for Mr. Lemaitre."

"Rather stand, ta," said Lemaitre, and in fact sat on the corner of Gideon's big, shiny desk. Several piles of paper stood on this, with three telephones, two ash trays, pen and ink, a blotting pad and several reference books, including *Whitaker's Almanack.* "Here it comes. Only two big jobs last night which kept us on the go this morning: murder of that old woman out at Ealing, and her missing lodger. He was picked up at Hammersmith and made a statement, all the usual stuff, he didn't mean to do it. I'd string him up without a trial if I had my way."

That kind of remark, made in front of a sergeant, was a clear indication of Lemaitre's frame of mind.

"The other job was the Milden Street jewel robbery, fifteen thousand quid's worth of stuff lifted, without a trace. We had every fence we know questioned today and haven't got a smell of the stuff. We don't even know who did the job. It had none of the usual trademarks; it was just neat and tidy and anonymous. There are the hangovers, too. Then—"

Lemaitre talked for ten minutes, touching upon dozens of different crimes, all of them large and important enough to have been brought to the Yard's notice, ranging from pocket picking to shoplifting, smash-and-grab to soliciting, fraud, embezzlement, attempted suicide, and causing grievous bodily harm— a kind of everyday's charge list which might have been lifted out of any issue of the *Police Gazette*. Lemaitre added odds and ends of information which were in the official report, one of the piles of papers on Gideon's desk. He smoked all the time, lighting one cigarette from the butt of another. Now and again Gideon signaled to the sergeant to make notes; otherwise he didn't interrupt. And he didn't light his pipe.

Lemaitre paused. Then:

"That's about the lot," he declared. "Shouldn't think it will break any records."

"What's this business of a Mrs. Penn who rang up three times to say she was worried about her husband because he hasn't been home for several weeks?"

"AB Division job," Lemaitre said. "Shouldn't think there's anything much in it; they sent a man round to talk to her. She's only been married a year or so, and just can't bear to think that her husband got tired of her and walked out so soon. But that's what he did all right, although she can't bring herself to believe it."

"Didn't you say she said she thought he must be dead?"

"That's what she *said.*"

"She give any reason?"

"If you ask me, she's right out of reason," Lemaitre opined. His one fault was his habit of jumping to conclusions; nothing seemed able to cure him. Before he could go on one of the telephones on Gideon's desk began to ring. Lemaitre looked at it with disgust, squashed out a cigarette and immediately began to light another; the tips of his forefinger and middle finger were so brown that they looked almost black. His eyes were tired, bloodshot and a little watery.

Gideon lifted up the receiver.

"Gideon," he said into it. "Who . . . Oh, yes, put him through." He covered the mouthpiece with his broad hand and said to the others. "AB Division."

"Perhaps hubby's come home," Lemaitre said sneeringly.

The truth about Lemaitre was that he needed a rest; somewhere quiet, somewhere on his own or with a wife who would fuss over him a little; and he wanted to be free from anxiety. And the truth about Lemaitre was that he'd married a bitch and, in spite of it, had never really fallen out of love with her. Lemaitre had failings but normally he was a sound man; now, he wasn't seeing anything straight because he was picturing his wife in another man's arms.

This was the first time Gideon had been really worried about him; he would have been, even without the Records man's comment.

A man came on the line.

"Gee-Gee? Elliott here. Just had a job which looks as if it could become nasty. Thought you'd better know at once. Kid disappeared from his home, Trenton Street, Chelsea. Four months old. Her mother left the baby in the kitchen while she talked to someone in the front room, and when she came back the kid was gone. Hell of a job."

"Any history?"

"That's all we know, yet."

"I'll put you through to Morley—he'll take all details—and I'll have a call out for the baby as soon as we can put it on the air and the teletype," Gideon promised. "That's all?"

20

"Yes."

"Anything more about a Mrs. Penn and her missing husband?"

"Just another poor kid with a husband who thinks he's Don Juan," said Elliott, and he wasn't prone to jumping to conclusions.

"Sure?"

"As near as I can be. Why?"

"I was looking through some reports on her yesterday," said Gideon, "and she seemed pretty levelheaded, not really the type to bury her head in the sand. Lem doesn't agree with me, but—"

"If she comes through again, I'll try to see her myself," Elliott promised.

"Thanks," said Gideon. "Now I'll put you through to Morley."

That only took a moment.

Next, he called the Information Room, told them about the missing baby and had them flash radio calls to all patrol cars. Soon the teletypes would be busy, all the Metropolitan Police and many in the Homes Counties would be on the lookout, for the one thing which always gave that little extra inducement to effort was the search for a missing child.

Gideon rang off, and another telephone rang promptly.

"Here we go," Lemaitre said, almost savagely. "Why don't they give us another pair of hands and ears?"

"Hello, Gideon here," said Gideon. "Yes, put him through . . . Hello, Mike . . . I haven't been in long but I gather they picked up the lodger, a man named Grey . . . Dunno how long he's lodged there, why? . . . Oh . . . *oh*. Yes, I'll see to it." He put down the receiver and motioned to the sergeant. "Take this down: Arthur Grey, suspect in the murder of Mrs. Sarah Allway of Giddons Road, Ealing, answers the description of a man calling himself Arthur Smith who disappeared from a house in Clapham three weeks ago after leaving his landlady for dead. Make a note that we want all details, and then telephone Hammersmith. Grey's still held there, isn't he?"

"No. Cannon Row," Lemaitre said shortly.

"Might be able to do it myself then," Gideon said. For the first time he lit his pipe, taking his time over it. It was cooler in the office, but just as smoky, and there was an acrid smell—the smell of smog—which rose above the smell of the tobacco. He nodded to the sergeant, who hurried out to type his notes so that Gideon could have them in front of him and copies could be sent out to other Departments and the Divisions. The smell, the smoke, the sight of Lemaitre's pale face and glassy eyes and the set of Lemaitre's lips did nothing to cheer Gideon up. When he had come into the office first Lemaitre and then the Prowler had been on top of his mind, but already there were signs that it might be a very bad night in a lot of ways.

A kidnapped infant, for a start.

A middle-aged man who lodged with elderly women and then attacked them.

Out in the dark city, within a radius of ten miles of this point, there were the professional criminals waiting to take their chance, there were people who had never committed a crime committing one now, there were the pros out in their hundreds, there was vice so thick that it stank, there was everything that would duly take its place in the crime statistics of the year; and there was Kate, the family—and young Matthew, probably still downstairs here with his eyes glistening, and Whittaker already so busy that he was wishing that he'd never set eyes on the boy.

There was the Prowler.

And Lemaitre.

*   *   *

22

For a few minutes the telephones were silent. Cars hooted outside as drivers became impatient with the fog, and on Charing Cross Bridge a train rumbled and a fog signal exploded with its mournful note of warning; the fog was really thick over the river.

Here, Lemaitre stood by his own desk shrugging himself into his coat.

"Lem, how are things at home?" Gideon asked, right out of the blue.

"Things at home are so good that one of these days you'll be charging me with murder," Lemaitre said. He forced a grin, fastened his collar and tie, and straightened his coat. His eyes were dark with shadows, his cheeks very lean; he had a bony chin. "Oh, forget it. Never has been a bed of roses—never been much bed at all, if you know what I mean! But there's no need for you to worry, George. Anything else I can do, before I go?"

"What do you expect to find when you get home?"

"A cold supper and an empty fireplace," said Lemaitre abruptly, "unless she's staying in because of the fog. She's taken to suspecting every man who looks at her on a foggy night as the Prowler. If she's home she'll tell me just what she thinks of me for leaving her all alone—oh, forget it, I said." But Lemaitre's smile was much too set. "Could get home and find her as sweet as honey, too. Sure there's nothing else?"

"No. Lem, thanks."

"See you the day after tomorrow, then," Lemaitre said. "So long."

Gideon said good night, Lemaitre went out, and the door closed behind him. It wouldn't be long before the night-duty inspector who would share the vigil with Gideon came back, but for a little while he had the office on his own. He lifted the receiver, put in a call to KI Division and, while he was waiting for it to come through, looked through the reports. Lemaitre had summarized them almost perfectly.

"Want me, Gee-Gee?" said the KI Divisional man.

"Oh, hello, yes." Gideon was so mild that he sounded almost uninterested. "Lemaitre's just left for home. Have a man on his street when he gets there, will you, and have someone find an excuse for calling on him in half an hour or so after he arrives."

"Sure," the Divisional man said, with complete understanding. "Any news about that baby?"

"No."

"Pity. If you don't find 'em quick you often don't find 'em at all, except in the river or under a foot of earth," the KI man observed; he was being factual, not callous. "Well, I'll fix that job in Lemaitre's street, and then see what's doing tonight. I hope the Prowler doesn't play any tricks on my beat."

"Let me know if he does," said Gideon dryly.

As he rang off, he warned himself ruefully that the Prowler was on top of everyone's mind. One reason was that no one was allowed to forget him. The evening newspapers had a paragraph about him whenever there was fog and there'd been a front-page story in tonight's *Evening Globe,* not much but just enough. It had repeated that the police had not yet caught the man known as the Prowler who, on foggy nights, would lie in wait for young girls, in the porches and the front doorways of their own homes, springing out on them, throttling them to silence and . . .

That was anyone's guess. The *Evening Globe* also pointed out, as if more in sorrow than in anger, that two things were known about the Prowler. He had once left a handkerchief of very good quality at the scene of an attack, and each girl who had seen him had talked of a "big shiny face"; presumably a mask of some kind. Neither of these clues had helped the police, nor had the descriptions of the Prowler given by the girls, for one had said "big and powerful," another had said "smallish" and several had plumped for "average size." Even ordinary witnesses to the same incident gave widely differing descriptions, and these girls had been cold with fear. But that didn't help.

It was also anyone's guess whether the Prowler would be out tonight. The fact that he'd been out seven times this autumn had been one of the reasons why Gideon had decided to come on nights for a week. He didn't expect to catch the Prowler on his first night, but he might see something which had been missed, or, when he got the early reports, might be able to suggest new moves against him.

A second reason for coming on nights was based on reports from the East End of increasing rivalry between the gangs of youths. Such rivalry could become ugly and create a serious situation, and Gideon wanted to keep his finger on its pulse.

In London itself the gangs operated only by night.

Now there was Mrs. Penn and her missing husband and her fears. There were dozens of Mrs. Penns and dozens of missing husbands, and only once now and again was it a police matter; usually it was just a case of a man, who, like Lemaitre, couldn't stand living at home any more. Or else the man was a callous beggar, who had no more interest in his wife.

There was the mother of the missing child.

There were dozens of other cases, some already reported and some still to come. Perhaps all of them would be quickly solved, or else would peter out; and perhaps one of them would become a sensation, perhaps a murder was lurking, perhaps that child was already dead.

The police would be on the lookout everywhere now.

It was a quarter past seven. The sergeant would soon be back, and Appleby, who was to work with Gideon for the night, ought to be here at any moment. Appleby was used to night work, an elderly, thoroughgoing man without much imagination but with a profound knowledge of his job and of the underworld. The C.I.D. would come to a standstill without its Applebys but—

Gideon scowled, for the telephone rang.

As he stretched out for the receiver, he had an odd feeling, almost a premonition of bad news, and he did not reckon to allow himself the luxury of such things. Perhaps it was because it was night, and there was the smoky fog outside, silence on the road and on the river, and silence in the passages, too.

"Gideon."

"Inspector Wragg of GH Division would like a word with you, sir."

"Put him through," said Gideon, and relaxed and grinned. Wragg was the man who had won promotion because of his interest in Greek gods and Roman relics. What a lot of bull one said to one's children sometimes! Had he sounded unbearably pompous? He'd meant to talk as man to man, but looking back felt that he'd laid the moralizing on with a trowel. Still, facts were facts, and Wragg—

"That you, Gee-Gee?" Wragg had a crisp voice.

"Yes."

"Thought I'd get straight on to you about this," said Wragg. "Had a teletype about the kidnapped baby ten minutes ago, and then only a few minutes after a kid was taken away from a car on my Division. Four-month-old boy. The mother's frantic."

As he listened, Gideon had the premonition again; this was going to be a night he wouldn't forget in a hurry.

3

The Baby Snatcher

The child lay in its cot, sleeping.

The room was warm. A faint glow of light came from beneath the door, and the sound of voices, which seemed a long way off, was just audible. Above it, soft and even, was the child's breathing.

Here was peace, with no knowledge of evil.

Sounds from the street came into the room from time to time: the beat of a car engine, the rattling of an old bicycle, three times in quick succession the staccato beat of a motorcycle engine which developed into a roar outside the window and then died away. Men and women walked, all briskly, in the cold night.

Then there came a sharper sound nearby, quick footsteps close to the window, followed by a clear ringing sound inside the house. Almost at once the distant voices stopped, a door opened, there were more footsteps, and these passed the door where the baby lay sleeping.

The front door opened.

"Oh, hello, Lucy!" a woman exclaimed, with obvious pleasure. "Come in a minute, dear."

"No, May, I'm not coming in," said the woman named Lucy. "Jim and me wondered if you and Fred would like to pop in for an hour. There's ever such a good program on the television. First there's Dobson and Young, *you* know—"

"Well, come in a minute, it's too cold to stand here," said May. "I'll ask Fred, and I expect he'll jump at it. Between you and me, dear, I don't think it will be long before we get the tele' ourselves. He's always moaning about not having it when everybody else has, but what with two children at grammar school and now Baby, it does seem an awful lot of money." The front door closed. "How would you like to have a look at Baby while I go and ask Fred?"

"Love to."

"He's a *pet*," said May in a softer voice, and there was a faint sound as the handle of the door turned. "That's what he is, an absolute *pet*. I put him down at half past six and as sure as I'm here he won't stir again until seven o'clock tomorrow morning. What about that for four months old?"

"You don't have to tell me," said Lucy.

The door opened, and light fell into the room but not directly onto the child, for the cot was behind the door so that bright light from the passage could not fall upon its eyes. They crept in, whispering, one woman short and with a mop of frizzy hair which showed up like twisted wire against the light, the other of medium height, plump with untidy dark hair. They stood at the head of the cot, just able to make out the dark head and the face, until the child's mother stretched out a hand and adjusted the blue woolen shawl a little, feeling the warm patch where the child's breathing fell.

"Bless him," she said in a voice what was almost choky with emotion. Then she turned and hurried out along the passage toward the kitchen and her husband.

There were voices from the kitchen, and then, clearly, May's voice:

"Oh, he'll be all right; he never *does* wake up. What's the matter with you tonight? We've done it before, haven't we?"

A gruff voice followed: "Oh, all right, if you really want to."

"If you'd rather stay here on your own with your nose stuck in a book, that's all right with me," said May, as if crossly. "I'll be just as welcome in my own."

"I said I'd come, didn't I?"

"You didn't sound as if you appreciated the kindness very much."

There was a pause; then a half-laughing "Oh, you," and May came hurrying, to have another look at her baby, and to draw Lucy into the passage.

"Fred's coming, dear. He always puts up this act. It's pride really; he doesn't like to think that if we want to see anything on the tele', we have to come next door for it. Read him like a book, I can. I'm just going to pop up to the bedroom and tidy my hair—"

"Oh, don't worry about your hair!"

"I couldn't let Jim see me in this mess; he'd start feeling sorry for Fred," said May, the dark-haired, younger woman. She turned and hurried up the stairs, calling back, "You can wait, dear. No, you go back to Jim, and Fred and me'll be along in a couple of jiffs."

"I'll wait," decided Lucy.

Fred came along, a stocky, gray-haired man with a smell of strong tobacco about him, and looking at the baby, smiling a gentle smile, and then they waited in the passage a little awkwardly until May came hurrying. Her hair didn't look much tidier, but she had dabbed on powder and lipstick, and was licking the tip of her forefinger and running it along the length of her eyebrows.

"Come on," she said. "All ready."

As she went out, she glanced round the front-room door. As Fred pulled the door behind him, he also glanced round. Then the door closed with a snap, there was a clatter of footsteps as they went out of one entry into another, voices, the opening and closing of the door.

All was quiet inside the house.

For some minutes, all was quiet in the street.

Then, from across the street, someone came walking.

It looked like a man of medium height, dressed in a big raincoat, a trilby hat and rubber-soled boots or shoes, and making little sound while walking; at most a soft, sliding sound. No one was in sight. It was a street with two rows of about fifty small, terraced houses on either side, each of two stories, and there were three lamps on either side. The lamp nearest the child's house was clearly visible, but the others were almost obscured by fog, which was much thicker now. A car passed the end of the street and its lights showed vaguely, but clear enough to show the smooth skin of a woman's face; this was not a man. The car disappeared as the shrouded woman reached the doorway of the child's house.

She bent down by the letter box, put her fingers inside and then groped gently, touched a piece of string, and pulled. There was a slight metallic sound as a key came out, tied to a string. She inserted the key quickly, pushed the door open and stepped inside, then closed the door without looking round.

She began to breathe hard, hissingly.

She leaned against the door for a moment, then straightened up as if with an effort, and walked toward the door of the front room, the passage leading to the kitchen, and the narrow staircase. She hesitated outside the door, then went up the stairs, quickly but with hardly a sound. There was enough light from the narrow hall to show the four doors leading off a small landing. She pushed each door open in turn, and shone a torch inside and the light fell upon beds, walls, furniture, a bathroom, handbasin, a mirror which flashed the brightness back; but this was not what the woman was seeking. She turned away and went downstairs, and hesitated again at the foot of the stairs, then turned toward the kitchen. Obviously there was nothing there, or in the tiny scullery, that she wanted. Two rooms remained: the front room and a smaller one next to it.

She opened the front-room door.

After a moment, she saw the cot and the child.

Her breathing became very heavy as she slipped the torch into her pocket, where it fitted snugly, and went close to the cot. Obviously she knew exactly what she wanted to do, and did not waste a moment. She pushed the bedclothes back, so that the baby lay wrapped in a blue blanket which enveloped all but his head, and lifted the bundle. She held it against her shoulder, one hand in the middle of its back as if she was quite familiar with it, and then pulled the shawl off at the top of the cot and wrapped it round the baby. This took only a few seconds, and soon the woman was stepping out of the room and into the passage, closing the door with her free hand. She took four strides to the front door, opened it and peered out.

A man and a woman, or boy and girl, passed on the other side of the street, and a motorcycle roared by.

The woman with the baby stepped into the foggy night and closed the door behind her with a snap. The house next door was in darkness, for the television was in a back room, out of sight and hearing of the street.

The child's eyes fluttered, but it did not wake.

The woman lowered it now, so that it was cradled in her arms, but didn't carry it with any outward pretense of affection; in fact she walked quickly, pumping the child up and down a little. Although the shawl was wrapped about the head, the little pink face was completely uncovered, and fog swirled about the mouth and nose.

Suddenly the baby coughed.

In the distance, there were the noises of the city.

"Well, thanks ever so, Lucy, and you, Jim," said May Harris. "It's been ever so nice, hasn't it, Fred? I enjoyed it very much."

"Best show I've seen for a long time," agreed Fred Harris, who looked as if he meant it.

He was red-faced with the warmth of the little room, where the television screen still showed its picture, but the sound had been turned down so that there was only a ghost voice which might have been a million miles away. May Harris was as flushed as her husband, her eyes were bright, her face was shiny as if she had not put a powder puff near it that evening, and her hair was a dark untidy mop. But there was merriment in her blue eyes, and much more character in her face than in Lucy Fraser's. Jim Fraser was an elderly man, nearly bald, with sharp features and a lot of deep lines at the eyes and mouth; he and his Lucy were fifteen years older than the Harrises.

"Glad you could come," Fraser said. "Sure you won't stay and have a cuppa?"

"Oh, I couldn't leave my baby any longer," said May Harris. "It isn't that I think he'd come to any harm, but you do hear of such things don't you? Fred, if you'd like to stay for a cup of char, I'll go and finish off that bit of ironing."

"Never outstay your welcome, that's what I always thought," said Harris. "They don't want us cluttering up the house."

He laughed, Fraser protested, May argued, Lucy went into the kitchen and put the kettle on. May was still protesting that they shouldn't stay when the tea was brought in, a large brown pot and white cups and saucers crowded on a small, wooden tray.

"Well, now it *is* made we may as well stay and have a cup," Harris conceded. "Like me to pop in and have a look at the brat, May?"

"Don't you call *my* child a brat!"

There was another general laugh as Harris went to the door. The house was identical with his own, and he could have found his way blindfolded. Once in the passage, he took out his pipe and lit it, as if he couldn't do without it for another moment. Then he went out, leaving the front door on the latch. The fog was much worse than when he had come here, and even the nearest street lamp was only a patch of misty light. The footsteps of people not far away seemed a long way off. In spite of the weather, he stood on the doorstep drawing at his pipe and adding smoke to the fog; then he strolled to his own house, let himself in with his own key, and noticed nothing at all unusual. The key on the string banged gently against the door. He didn't go into the front room at first but along to the kitchen, where he put some coal on the fire which heated the hot-water boiler behind the fireplace.

Then he went to the front room.

He opened the door softly, crept in, saw the foot of the cot, let his gaze shift quickly toward the pillow— and caught his breath. For a moment, he did not seem to be breathing at all. Then:

"God!" he gasped.

He spun round and switched on the light, not knowing what he expected to find. There were the bedclothes, turned down as if his wife had lifted the baby out, but—nothing else.

He made a strangled sound.

He pushed the cot away from the wall, as if he feared that by some miracle the child in swaddling clothes had been able to climb out of the cot and had landed on the floor close to the wall. There was just a blank space. For a moment he stood as if he had lost the power to move, but suddenly he turned round, reached the passage and called in a loud voice:

"Jackie! Millicent!"

There was no answer.

He hesitated, his hands clenching, turning his head this way and that—and then, as if driven by some compulsion which he could not resist, dashed up the stairs. He made the walls shake and the staircase quiver in his fear as he called again:

"Jackie! Millicent!"

There was still no answer.

All the rooms were empty—his and May's, the tiny room where the child slept during the night, the room with two beds, which Jacqueline and Millicent shared. His daughers were out, he didn't expect them back until half past ten; there was a nearby school-and-youth club they went to every Tuesday.

He stood on the little landing, a stocky man with graying hair, a big face, his clenched fists raised at chest height, an expression of bewilderment touched with horror on his face and in his honest gray eyes. He licked his lips.

"I can't—" he began.

Then he gulped, and started down the stairs, and as he went he said in a hoarse whispering voice:

"May, what'll *May* say?

"It can't have happened, I must be—"

He broke off.

He went into the front room again, where the light was so bright and the cot was empty, and he knew that it was coldly, cruelly true. He stared at the door, lips set tightly and pipe forgotten. He heard sounds, without knowing what they were. The dazed, horrified expression was still in his eyes as at last he moved toward the door.

"May," he said chokily. "Oh, God."

Then the front door was pushed open, and his wife appeared, still flushed and obviously anxious and alarmed. Fred stopped, quite still. He did not need to speak, for his face told her of reasons for great dread. Her expression, already anxious, changed to one of sudden alarm, but not yet with fear or horror. She moved quickly toward him gripping his right hand tightly.

"Fred, what is it? I heard you shouting. What—"

He tried to speak, but could not.

"Why don't you say something instead of just standing there?" cried May. "Why—"

Then—and it was only a few seconds after she had entered the passage—the significance of the open front-room door and the bright light inside seemed to strike her. All color drained from her cheeks. She pushed her husband to one side and ran into the room. She stared at the cot, her hands raised, her mouth wide open, and the light from the ceiling shone upon her eyes and seemed to put stark terror into them.

She jerked her head round to look at her husband. She could not speak. There was a moment of awful silence, and then tall Jim Fraser spoke from the porch.

"Everything all right there?"

"Fred," May said, in a queer little voice, "it can't

35

have happened. It can't, it—oh my *baby*. Where's my baby? Why did you shout—*Jackie! Millie!*" She swung round suddenly toward her husband, saying as if to herself. "They're home early, they've taken—"

"I've looked—" Fred began, and choked. "Looked—everywhere."

May didn't speak.

Jim Fraser appeared in the doorway, sparse and thin and old looking and puzzled.

"Everything is all right, isn't it?" he began, and then saw them and realized that horror was here. Quite suddenly he became a different man from the elderly, easygoing neighbor who was always ready to lend a hand. His voice became firmer and touched with authority as he moved forward, going on: "Here, what's up? What are you looking like that for, May?" He glanced toward the cot and immediately understood, and his voice became even more authoritative. "Say you've looked everywhere, Fred?"

"Y-yes. Y-yes, I—"

"My baby," said May Harris, in that queer little hurt voice. "Who's taken my baby?"

"Fred, nip next door and tell Lucy that she's wanted here," said Fraser. "Tell her to make it snappy. Then go along to the phone box at the corner of Grettley Street, and dial nine-nine-nine. I'll look after May while you're gone, don't worry. Looks as if someone just picked the baby up, doesn't it. No sign that anyone did it any harm, is there? Lot of funny things happen, and babies usually turn up. Come on, Fred, get a move on."

Thus he averted panic, then.

*   *   *

36

Appleby had arrived at Gideon's office, a clean-shaven man with gray hair which he kept short, a fresh complexion, rather bright, beady, glittering gray eyes, a thin-cheeked man with a long nose, a big mouth and, by reputation, a sense of humor; the kind of humor that put tacks on chairs. He was a Cockney who spoke with a nasal twang he had never quite overcome, and he was reputed to know more thieves' slang and Cockney rhyming slang than anyone else in the Force. He had come in almost flustered, not realizing that Gideon would be in his own office, and expecting him at the office of the Chief Superintendent usually on duty at night. Now he had settled down at Lemaitre's desk, with dozens of papers spread out in front of him, looking much more like a busy bookmaker than a C.I.D. man.

"Sorry, old pal, I must be slipping."

"My fault, Charley," Gideon said. "I forgot to send a message saying I'd be here—couldn't come to your office, as far as that goes, but now you're here we'll call it a day. Or a night." He grinned as he sat back in his big chair and looked across at Appleby. "I haven't heard you say it yet."

Appleby looked puzzled.

"Say what?"

"Who it's a good night for."

Appleby gave a quick smile.

"Oh, the Prowler. Got the Prowler on the brain, some of these people, but I admit I'll have more peaceful nights when the swine's inside. Real trouble with the Prowler isn't the harm he does by scaring the wits out of these kids. Oh, it's bad enough, but—you want to know something?"

"Always ready to listen."

"One night last week we had *twenty-seven* blasted calls through nine-nine-nine to say that the Prowler had been seen," Appleby said, "and we had to make *twenty-seven* bloody investigations on a night when it took every patrol car and Squad car we had twice as long as usual to get around in the fog. The Prowler does a hell of a lot more damage stopping us from getting on with other jobs than he does to these girls."

"You might sing a different tune if you had daughters of your own, Charley."

"Coupla sons have been quite enough for me and the old china to handle," Appleby said without arguing. "Funny business, these babies, isn't it? Two snatched."

"You know how things often run in pairs," Gideon remarked, more to get Appleby's reaction than anything else. Being close to his pension often seemed to blunt a man's approach to his jobs, made him fall back on routine and the conventional approach, which often saved a lot of trouble.

"I know how they run in quintuplicate sometimes," said Appleby dryly, "but these two babies were snatched within a few hundred yards of each other on the same evening. One from the southern edge of GH Division, one from the northern edge of AB Division. If you ask me, that's one for the curiosity stakes."

"I'm with you there," Gideon said. "Hope we don't get a third. Anything else look worth special attention?"

"Not yet," said Appleby, "but the night's hardly started."

"Don't I know it," agreed Gideon, and got up. "Been down to the Information Room lately?"

"Half an hour ago. Your young hopeful was still there."

"I'll nip down and have a word with him, and if he's still hanging around I'll send him home," said Gideon. "Won't be long, but I might pop into the canteen on the

38

way back."

"Have one for me," said Appleby.

So he was alert, apparently right up to his job, and as zestful as a man fifteen or twenty years his junior; Gideon decided that, if there was a weakness in the night operation at the Yard, it didn't lie in any slackening of Charley Appleby's keenness.

At his normal slow, deliberate gait Gideon walked toward the stairs. The lift wasn't at this landing, so he walked down; it was only two flights. The ground floor had the deserted look which he didn't relish, but as he reached the Information Room it was like going out of the shadow into sunshine. The big room was well lit. The uniformed men with their long rakes, like croupiers at four green baize tables, were all moving little blocks of wood which represented the patrol cars in the districts they covered. Each table represented one of the four Districts of Metropolitan London, and each was an administrative area. There were small colored counters showing the spots where crimes had been reported that evening.

Several men sitting at the radio transmitter, with earphones on, were at ease just then, and lounging against the front of the transmitter was young Matthew, who hadn't yet noticed his father. Whittaker was in his small office, talking on the telephone. Teletype machines clattered busily, recording messages from magic, silent voices, and strangely disembodied sounds came faintly into the room.

A sergeant sitting by the receiver said:

"Here's a call."

Matthew straightened up eagerly, and still didn't notice his father. The big clock on the wall showed that it was nearly half past nine; the large second hand ticked round abruptly every second.

"May I—" Matthew began.

"Yes, put 'em on." The operator motioned to a spare pair of headphones, and then said briskly. "Scotland Yard." Matthew jammed the headphones on, his eagerness really something to see; how like Kate the boy looked sometimes!

Then, his eyes lost their brightness. His lips set. He made no attempt to get the headphones off, but obviously he didn't like what he heard.

The operator kept saying, "Yes ... Yes ... Yes," and made written notes, swiftly. Gideon stepped behind him and tried to read the notes, but they were in shorthand and he didn't know the system which was used.

"Yes, we'll send at once," said the operator. "You are Mr. Frederick Harris, of twenty-seven Hurdle Street, Fulham, and while you were next door at a neighbor's house your four-month-old child was taken from your house. . . . Yes, Mr. Harris, we'll have someone with you in a very few minutes, and we'll do everything we can."

He rang off.

"That's *three*," he said, and the tone of his voice matched the look on Matthew's face.

Matthew had seen Gideon now, was staring at him.

"Hurdle Street, Fulham," Gideon repeated, as if to himself. "That's CD Division and not far from the other two snatch jobs." He nodded at Matthew, and then moved toward a long counter and picked up a telephone. "Give me Mr. Appleby, he's in my office. . . . Hello, Charley, another baby's been stolen, CD Division this time. I think I'll go over myself and see how things are. Flash me if you want me."

"Righto," said Appleby.

"Come on, Matt," Gideon said to his son as he put the receiver down. "You can come with me as far as

40

Wandsworth Bridge Road, and can walk home from there. Won't be a couple of jiffs." He moved his massive body very swiftly, and went to Whittaker's office. Messages were being flashed to patrol cars in the Hurdle Street area; in a few moments the Division would be called, then the teletype messages to the other Divisions would start going out. Here was a major task, and somehow that showed in the attitude of all the men down here, in the way the rakes were pushed about, in the attitude of the men sitting at the radio.

"I'll get everything done, George," Whittaker said.

"Thanks. And try this—send someone from GH and AB over to Hurdle Street. Each must be a chap who's been working on the baby-snatch job in his Division. We want to find out similarities and all that kind of thing. Who's on duty at AB?"

"Dixon."

"He won't lose any time," said Gideon. "Dixon and Wragg, hmm. Tell 'em I'll be there."

"Okay," said Whittaker.

"Come on, Matt," said Gideon. "I—"

He stopped in the middle of what he was going to say. A new message was coming in, a distant voice sounded clearly, and two of the radio operators glanced at each other in a swift, meaningful way which told its own story. Matthew watched. Whittaker was already on the telephone but was looking out of his office.

An operator said, "Okay, right away." He turned to look at one of the District map tables. "Smash-and-grab raid at Kilber's in Hatton Gardens. One of our men injured trying to stop the car's getaway."

"Okay," the patrol-car said, and began to put out the messages.

Gideon put a hand on one man's shoulder.

"When Mr. Whittaker's off the telephone, ask him to

41

call Mr. Appleby, in my office, to have Hatton Gardens checked. Seems a queer place for a night smash-and-grab job to me. Better have the street and district cordoned off."

"Right, sir."

"Come on, Matthew," Gideon said, and this time they got out of the room without being interrupted.

4

Common Factors

It was much foggier in the yard than when they had arrived, and the Embankment lights were all invisible, little more than pale haloes in the murk. But it wasn't the kind of fog to keep traffic to a standstill; there was at least a fifty-yard visibility. Squad cars were on the move, engines roaring, the carbon monoxide from their exhausts smelling strong and unpleasant on the fog-laden, windless air. Yellow fog lights shone on the fog, cars passed and Gideon got into his own, making the body sway to one side with his fifteen stones, and Matthew got in the other. Doors slammed.

"Listen, Matt," Gideon said, "I've got a lot on my mind and I'm not going to talk much, but don't let that worry you."

"No, I won't."

"You've had a quick look at what the job can be like," went on Gideon. "Sometimes it goes on like that right through the night, but often nothing very big comes of it. We've got this baby-snatching job tonight and we don't like it. It'll be all right if we get the babies back but hell if we don't. The job can be hell. There are times when I've hated what's happened."

"I can understand that," Matthew said gruffly.

"Good. Here's another thing you ought to bear in mind. That radio operator used shorthand. He can also speak Italian, Spanish, Russian, Greek and Dutch. There's bound to be someone with the Scandinavian languages and someone else in the building who knows others. You can't know too much, and you can always find a use for what you know."

"I could see that, too," said Matthew thoughtfully. "Especially about the shorthand. I thought the only decent job you needed shorthand for was journalism. One of them did hold a long conversation in a language I didn't understand, too."

"Well, you kept your eyes and ears open, anyway. On the whole, did you enjoy it?"

Matthew didn't reply at once, and so puzzled Gideon, but it was too difficult to drive to allow him a glance at the boy. He turned round Parliament Square as a bus loomed up dangerously close, and he let it push its way ahead.

"I didn't just enjoy it," Matthew said quietly. "I was fascinated, Dad. I want to be a policeman more than ever."

Gideon said, "Well, don't be in too much of a hurry." He was wondering what Kate would say and what he ought to do. Matthew had undoubted brilliance, and a scholastic flair. The Force wasn't exactly what he'd had in mind for the boy.

He couldn't think about it then, anyway.

Fifteen minutes later, Matthew got out of the car to walk toward Hurlingham, and Gideon turned into a narrow side street which took him to Hurdle Street and the disaster which had struck at Number 27.

*　　*　　*

It was never possible to tell how human beings would react under this kind of savage pressure and shock. The mother's reaction might vary from shrieking hysterics to cold, frightening quiet. The best reaction was tears developing into words which wouldn't stop. As Gideon approached the front door at 27 Hurdle Street he heard a woman talking so fast that it was difficult to distinguish the words. If that was Mrs. Harris, it was a good thing.

The street was crowded with police cars. Neighbors were out in strength, in spite of the biting cold and the fog. Front doors were wide open, light streamed from them into the street, and from windows also; yet there were places where it was impossible to see across the road. Policemen and the public made shadowy figures. People were coughing; someone gave half a dozen loud sneezes.

Inside the front room was Wragg, of GH Division, a man not unlike Appleby to look at, but with jet black hair smoothed down glossily over his smallish head, and a black mustache. In the room with him were photographers, fingerprint men and two others who were taking measurements of the position of the cot. There was a tall, bald-headed man and a short, stocky one—the stocky man had the hurt baffled look of a distracted father.

The woman was talking somewhere else in the house.

Wragg flashed a quick smile; he had very white teeth.

"Hello there," he greeted. "I thought you wouldn't be long. These chaps don't need telling anything, though." He glanced at a portly man standing by the window of the little, crowded room; that was Willy Smith, of CD Division. "We had a message just now that a chap who was on the baby job at AB will be here soon, too."

"Good," said Gideon. "Who's the father—stocky chap?"

"Yes. The other chap's a neighbor, named Fraser."

It was like Wragg to hand out information wherever he was, and like Willy Smith to let him; there was no false Divisional pride in Willy. He grinned at Gideon, but behind the grin there was anxiety for this man and his wife and the stolen child.

"How'd it happen?"

Wragg explained briefly and comprehensively.

"How'd the snatcher get in?" asked Gideon quietly.

"Well, they have a key on a piece of string just inside the door; you can hook it out through the letter box. Thousands of people do that. It doesn't help to tell them it's inviting trouble. Looks as if the key was hooked out, anyway. No prints on the door; no scratches, either. But the front-room window's open a couple of inches. He could have come in that way, too."

"I see," said Gideon, and stepped to Harris' side.

"Mr. Harris?"

Harris looked up almost blankly, and nodded.

"I'm from Scotland Yard," Gideon said quietly, "and I would like you to know that we shall do everything humanly possible to get the child back before the night is out. I expect the others have asked you to try to think of everything that might help us."

Harris nodded again. He looked rather like a man who was punch drunk, and didn't quite know where he was or what was going on. He wasn't likely to be any help to anyone. The chief hope lay in the neighbor or in the child's mother. There was no point in talking to her now—while she was talking nineteen to the dozen just inside the kitchen.

"Place to talk next door," Willy Smith volunteered. "I fixed it with Fraser."

"Let's go," said Gideon

The room looked in turmoil, the street looked like the scene after an accident, but in fact the situation was completely under control, and no time was wasted. Gideon was used to the matter-of-fact way in which the men went about their job, the quiet questions, the unflurried search for fingerprints, footprints, anything that might give the slightest help. Plain-clothes men were questioning the neighbors, too, trying to find anyone who had been in the street during the time that the Harrises had been out of their house. More policemen were on duty outside Number 29, and as Gideon went inside he had to duck, the top of the doorway was so low.

Here, the front room was better furnished, and obviously little used. The light was bright, and a gas fire hissed and glowed more yellow than red.

"I was on the snatch that we had earlier," Wragg said. "House in Field Street, much the same type as this. Young parents, named Dean. First child, four months old, asleep in a 'carricot' in the back of their little car. They were out shopping, and parked the car in a side street near their road. They say they weren't away for ten minutes, but when they got back the baby was gone. By the time I got there, the mother was in hysterics. Still is, probably."

"Any leads?"

"None at all, but—" Wragg stopped as there was a tap at the door and a big, burly-looking, youngish man appeared with a shock of gingery hair, red cheeks and bright blue eyes. He was wearing a new-looking overcoat and he stood at attention.

"Mr. Gideon, sir?"

"Yes," said Gideon, "You from AB Division?"

"Yes, sir. Detective Sergeant Hill."

"You were on the spot at the baby-snatching job, weren't you?" asked Gideon, and motioned Hill further into the room. He closed the door before obeying, and obviously regarded Gideon with awe. He had very

47

large hands and long arms, and he looked astounded when Gideon offered him a cigarette from a fat silver case, kept for offering.

"If you don't mind, sir, I won't just now—never smoke except when I'm at home."

"Good rule," said Gideon. "Let's have the story, will you?"

Hill told it in detail yet with no waste of words. The AB Divisional case ran more parallel to the Hurdle Street kidnapping than the kidnapping from the car. A four-month-old baby boy had been asleep in the kitchen of a small house, and his mother had been in the front of the house, talking with the minister of a local nonconformist church. Entry had been through the back door, which had been approached through a small back yard in turn approached from a service alley. It had been the first of the three kidnappings, and had first been discovered at half past six.

"So what is there in common?" asked Gideon quietly. "Give me yours again, Mr. Wragg, will you?"

Wragg did, succinctly.

Gideon nodded at Willy Smith, who gave the details, as known, of the kidnapping here in Hurdle Street.

"Have a go, Hill, and see what common factors you find," Gideon said.

"I'd rather leave it to you, sir."

His deferential manner, very near to obsequiousness, was beginning to irritate Gideon, but he didn't show it. Nor did Willy Smith; but Wragg looked with obvious impatience at the sergeant from the neighboring Division.

"All right," said Gideon. "Each baby was male. Each was about four months old. Each was healthy. Each was in a room or a car, asleep. Each job was done between six o'clock and nine fifteen tonight. Each was in this part of London; the place of kidnapping was probably within the radius of a mile from the place where GH, AB and CD Divisions meet. Each was the child of parents in more or less the same social and financial position—each family has enough money to rub along with but, as far as we yet know, none of them is wealthy—not wealthy enough to pay a fat ransom, for instance." Gideon paused, and it seemed as if that was for breath as much as anything else. "Each appears to have been a happy family, and the father as badly upset as the mother. Each kidnapping might have been done with some knowledge of where the baby was likely to be at a certain time—it's not certain that these were all chance kidnappings, as they would have been if all the jobs had been by day, and the babies taken from outside shops or houses. No sign of violence in any case; all cots and bedclothes undisturbed. So far, no evidence in any case whether the kidnapper was a man or woman."

Gideon stopped, as if he'd finished this time.

"Another thing," Willy Smith put in dryly. "Only a madman would do a thing like this. Man or woman."

Gideon didn't comment. Hill was having difficulty in keeping his big hands still; obviously he was likely to be ill at ease all the time he was in Gideon's presence. Wragg said abruptly:

"Could be a looney, but—"

There was a flurry of movement outside, and after a brief pause someone tapped sharply at the door. Gideon, his back to the fire, was beginning to feel too hot, and was also feeling uneasy because so far there was nothing at all that could be construed as a lead to the kidnapper.

"Come in."

It was a plain-clothes detective sergeant from the Yard.

"Hello, Rasen, what's up?" asked Gideon.

"Thought you'd better know this at once, sir," said the sergeant. "Young chap outside has been riding round the block on his motorbike a lot tonight. He had it new—new second hand, that is—yesterday, and meant to ride it, fog or no fog. He says he was pulled in at the curb with engine trouble just round the corner in Grettley Street—the end of this street, sir—when he saw a man coming round the corner carrying a baby. This was about twenty past eight."

"Ah," breathed Gideon. "Any description?"

"Smallish, and wearing a raincoat and a trilby hat, sir."

"That's all?"

"The best I could get," Rasen said.

"Sure it was a man?"

"The motorcyclist says so, sir."

Hill's eyes were glistening and his hands stopped fidgeting. Willy Smith clapped his hands, and Wragg was eager.

"Now we're looking for a smallish man seen with a baby near the other two places," Gideon said. "Hill, use one of the radio cars outside to contact your Division and put out that description, will you?"

"Yes, sir!" Hill went hurrying.

"Gor, where do they get 'em from these days?" Wragg almost exploded, but he was also on the way to the door.

"Hold it," said Gideon sharply. "We're looking for something else. Three baby kidnappings in one evening, out of the blue, add up to someone who isn't normal. Why should anyone take three in a row? We're looking for a motive, or else we're looking for a maniac."

"Where does that get us?" Wragg asked reasonably.

"Dunno," said Gideon, "but it's something to think about, and we might pick up a lead."

"Right," said Wragg. "Motive or mania!"

"Right," said Willy Smith.

They went out together.

Gideon felt a sense of frustration, even of anger with himself, because he could do so little, and nothing really quickly. He asked himself the questions again: why had the babies been kidnapped—three children of parents who were unknown to one another? It seemed certain that the three kidnappings had been by the same individual, and he didn't like to take refuge behind the "mania" theory.

The need for a motive nagged at him.

It would nag at Wragg and Smith, too, and one of them might get an idea. In any case, just by being here he had gingered them up, and they would be on their mettle—Division working against Division, too. A little competition wouldn't do any harm. He hadn't really wasted a journey, and had seen again the thing that he had seen hundreds, even thousands of times before, and which never failed to make him hopeful.

The police, at work.

Within half an hour policemen by the hundreds would be questioning people in the neighborhood of the three places from which the babies had been kidnapped. The motorcyclist's lead might be decisive. He'd talked to young Matthew about the uses of general knowledge, but hadn't mentioned the advantages of thoroughness for detail and Lady Luck.

He went out into the passage, then into the street, seeing the crowd, the cars, the wreathing mist, the pale yellow lights—and then hearing a voice quite clear above the rumble of conversation.

"Hear what he said? They found the kid, dead."

When he first heard that, Gideon was just outside the Frasers' house. By the time he had walked ten paces he

51

had heard it a dozen times, sometimes whispered, often spoken in a loud, clear voice. It traveled from speaker to speaker and was taken up on the instant, as a cheer is taken up among crowds lining a street to see some great celebrity. Gideon's first reaction was to reject it, but he was in no position to reject or accept; so far it was simply rumor.

He came upon the Flying Squad man, Detective Inspector Rasen, and asked gruffly:

"Is it true? The child's been found?"

"Don't know anything about it myself, sir." Rasen looked about the crowd distastefully. "Lot of ghouls, that's what they are."

"Get the story checked, will you?"

"Yes, right away." The Flying Squad man called his car crew, and in turn they called the police who were questioning the crowd. In a few minutes Gideon felt better; it had been a rumor, and was soon tracked down to its source, a man who had said, "Wouldn't it be awful if they found the baby dead?" But the rumor and the speed with which it had traveled had robbed Gideon of any hope of peace of mind. He went back to 27 Hurdle Street, feeling bleak and depressed. All the photographs, of the fingerprints and the baby's cot had been taken; there seemed little hope of getting a line from anything found there.

The woman was no longer talking.

Gideon knew that he need not stay. He had come to see how the job was being handled, and couldn't really handle it himself, could only set the pace. He'd set it, and would be much more use back at his desk; yet he was hesitant about going, and stood in the little passage, big and massive and powerful looking, aware that several Yard and Divisional officers were looking at him and wondering what he was going to do.

Two men, Harris and his neighbor Fraser, were in

the kitchen. The door was ajar. A man, probably Harris, was talking in a despairing kind of voice, protestingly. Gideon took a step nearer.

"I don't care what you say," a woman said. "If they don't find my baby, I'll do away with myself. Life just wouldn't be worth living."

Gideon turned to a man just behind him.

"Anyone sent for a doctor?"

"Not to my knowledge, sir."

"See it's done, will you—find out the name of the Harrises' family doctor first."

"Yes, sir."

"May, dear," another woman was saying anxiously, "it's no use talking like that, honestly, and in any case—"

"If they don't find my baby, I'll do away with myself," the mother said. "I shouldn't have gone out and left him, that's the truth. It was my fault. It wasn't anyone else's fault, it was my fault. Fred didn't want to come. It's no use saying anything, Fred. You were sitting in that chair with that book in your hands, and you didn't want to come out, so it was my fault. And all because of a rotten television program, too. I risked my baby's life all because of that; it's my fault."

Gideon pushed open the door.

He almost filled the doorway, and his very bulk made the others stare at him. The dumpy, frizzy-haired woman was startled; the dark-haired taller woman with a mask-like face and desperately glittering eyes looked as if it didn't matter if the devil walked in. She was sitting on an upright chair, with her husband just behind her. The neighbor's husband was standing by the window.

"Mrs. Harris?" asked Gideon quietly.

She stared.

"You haven't—" began Harris unexpectedly, and the

tone of his voice seemed to transform his wife. She sprang to her feet and flung herself at Gideon, and in that shattering moment Gideon realized that he had done the one unforgivable thing; he had given the parents unjustified hope. The woman clutched his hands, and she was trembling; and he cursed himself for having pushed open the door.

"I just came to tell you that hundreds of policemen will be searching for your child within the next hour, Mrs. Harris, and that we shall do everything it's humanly possible to do."

He had meant to try and take her mind off despair; instead, he had cast her more deeply into it. She dropped her hands. She seemed to stop trembling. She turned back to her husband, who put his arms round her shoulders and stared at Gideon as if pleading with him to go before he did more harm.

All a man could do was try.

And within a mile of this house, two other families knew this same grief.

But now, facts were building up. Wax polish on the floor beneath the partly open windows had a shiny surface which hadn't been smeared that night, so the kidnapper had used a key—probably the one hanging in the letter box. There was a chance that the kidnapper knew that a key was kept there—and obviously many neighbors knew that. So all the neighbors would have to be questioned quickly and closely. The right way to deal with the Harrises was to give them plenty to think about, too, and to let them help with the investigation.

Willy Smith came up.

"Wouldn't be someone who'd lost a child, and was looking for him, would it?" he asked almost apologetically. "I've just been thinking about the Postlewaite case, when a woman lost her own child—natural causes, if you remember—and wouldn't believe it was dead. She went round taking other babies out of their prams, and when stopped with one, swore it was her own." When Gideon didn't answer, Smith went on: "Don't you remember? About seven years ago, and—"

"Oh, I remember," said Gideon. "I'm just wondering if you've got something there. Try it, Willy. Check with the Registrars of Births and Deaths, find out if anyone living near the Harrises has lost a baby recently. The weakness is that a *man* wouldn't be likely to be affected, but the mother—"

"We've been told it was a man."

"I know, but try it. That motorcyclist might have made a mistake in the dark."

"I'll send a man round to the Registrar of Births at once; that won't take long. If we have a bit of luck we might get a break soon. Any special way you want us to handle the job?"

"Your way," said Gideon.

"Thanks." Smith looked up at him with a half-smile. "I'll see you get all the news as it comes in. There's a chap from the *Evening Globe* outside, by the way. Any special angle?"

"Don't think so," said Gideon. "The more publicity we get on this job, the better."

"Taking the very words out of my mouth," said Smith.

Gideon went to his car, and wasn't surprised to see another one just behind it, marked *Press*. No one stood near and he hadn't yet been recognized. He got into the car and drove off. Two policemen had to clear a way for him, there were so many people about. The fog seemed to have lifted a little just here, too; he could see the curious faces more clearly. Ghouls? If they started another rumor and it reached Mrs. Harris, they would be more than ghouls.

He flicked on his radio.

"Gideon here—any messages?"

"No special messages for you, sir, but we've just had a flash from Hatton Gardens."

"Go on."

"The smash-and-grab was a decoy raid, drew two of our chaps off a burglary a hundred yards away, but we caught the lot." There was a deep satisfaction in the speaker's voice. "Two were involved in the smash-and-grab, two others found on enclosed premises."

"Fine! Where was it?"

"Marks and Sanders," the man said.

The firm of Marks and Sanders was one of the largest diamond merchants in Hatton Gardens. The premises had an elaborate burglarproof system and a fortune in precious stones was usually kept in its strong room. Well, that was a score to him. Four men on a charge, a burglary stopped, and a success to give the men at the Yard an added incentive. It might all have happened in exactly the same way if he hadn't sent that message through to Appleby; but it might not. . . .

He turned a corner, and a few yards along found that the fog was even thicker than it had been early on; so it was patchy, and was moving from place to place. What he wanted was a good steady fifteen-mile-an-hour wind that would shift the damned stuff.

He crawled along at twenty miles an hour. Two people passed, and he could hear what they said quite clearly. The radio kept crackling, but he didn't turn it off. It was after ten, but the night had hardly started. God knew what was going on behind this blanket of fog—how many people were frightened, how many people were in a kind of terror, how many were planning some crime, how many—

"What you want is a whisky and soda," Gideon said aloud and he promised himself he would have one as soon as he reached the Yard. But he didn't go straight up to the canteen; he went to the office, and opened it to find Appleby and the brown-clad sergeant together. He didn't like Appleby's expression.

"What's up?" asked Gideon sharply.

"They found the body of the first baby in a Fulham garden, not far from where it was taken," Appleby said. "Suffocated."

This time it was true.

5

The Prowler

Gideon sat alone at his desk half an hour afterward. Appleby had gone down to the canteen for a cup of tea. The office was blessedly quiet, and the telephone hadn't rung for fifteen minutes, but it would soon. Downstairs there was little doubt that the Information Bureau was getting really busy. Every mean little crook in London would see his chance tonight, and it wasn't cold enough to keep them indoors.

The important, in fact the essential thing was to keep a sense of balance. One had to. Most of the time it was easy enough, but when something happened like tonight, the sense of balance could be too easily disturbed; one could see life as one sordid tragedy after another, instead of getting a true perspective.

The telephone rang.

"Here it goes," Gideon thought, and lifted the receiver. "Yes."

"Mrs. Gideon's on the line, sir."

"Put her through," said Gideon.

If this had been by day, the call would have surprised him; Kate seldom called. Was there some kind of family emergency? His thoughts ran quickly, but evenly enough, over the possibility. Matthew hadn't been fool enough to stay out, had he? He was uneasy about Matthew, not sure that he had helped him.

"Hello, George."

"Hello, Kate." His anxiety didn't sound in his voice.

"I wondered if you'd be in."

No emergency, then. What was it?

"I know where I'm best off," said Gideon. "The office is as warm as toast, and—"

"What have you been doing to Matthew?"

"Eh?"

"You heard me," Kate said.

He could picture her sitting by the telephone in the kitchen, where there was an extension. She was probably on the arm of his chair, wearing a black skirt and white blouse, a full bosomed, handsome woman with a gleam in her eyes, a good complexion and an air of great competence.

"All I did was to let him have a look round at the Information Room."

"If you'd given him a hundred pounds, you couldn't have pleased him more. He's been going round with his head in the clouds ever since he got back—it's the first night I've ever known when he didn't want any supper!"

Gideon chuckled.

"What I really told him was that I wanted him to go all out for that university scholarship."

"That I don't believe," said Kate. "I—just a minute."

She put the telephone down on the table by the chair; for a few minutes he heard nothing. He smiled at the thought that Kate had called up just for a chat; for it amounted to that. It went deeper, of course, and Matthew had made the reason clear. She was edgy when her George was out at night, and needed a kind of reassurance, and—

Something seemed to hit Gideon a savage blow.

Years ago, Kate and he had lost a child, one about the dead baby's age. He had been out, after Kate had pleaded with him to stay. That had begun an estrangement which only the years had broken down; and tonight there were three babies, one dead and two in danger. Until this minute he hadn't thought of that.

"George?"

"Hello, I'm sill here."

There was a note of laughter in Kate's voice.

"It was Matthew. He found that he was hungry after all. Apparently you didn't do him any serious harm. What did he talk about?"

"Where is he now?"

"In the larder, foraging."

"Well, don't let him know that you know yet," said Gideon. "This fancy might fade out. He wants to give up the idea of a university, and join the Force as a copper."

Gideon paused, but Kate didn't respond immediately, and he went on more quickly and a little anxiously. "He has a silly notion that the life is adventurous and romantic, and I tried to make sure that he knows that it could be dull."

"I don't know what you tried to do, but you succeeded in making him think that our policemen are wonderful—even including his father," Kate said, quite normally. "I've suspected for some time that he didn't want to sit for the examination, but"—she was anxious after all—"can't we persuade him that he'd be more use at the Yard as a lawyer than—"

"A flatfoot," Gideon said dryly. "We'll have a damned good try. Anything else, Kate?"

"Not really," Kate said, and then added almost brusquely. "What kind of a night is it up there?"

"Bit misty," Gideon said promptly.

"I know you and a 'bit misty,'" Kate said roundly. "It wouldn't be thick here and thin by the river, but I didn't mean that. I meant are you busy?"

"Busyish," said Gideon, and hesitated, and realized more clearly and without the sense of shock that the reason that he had gone to Hurdle Street was because of the death of his own child so many years ago. Subconscious compulsion. In the morning, Kate would open her newspaper and read the headlines, and if he didn't tell her now, she would probably think that he had deliberately kept it back from her. So: "One very ugly job," he told her.

"Oh."

"Looks like a psychopathic case," Gideon went on. "Three young babies have been kidnapped." He needn't tell her that one of them was dead.

She was momentarily quiet again. Then:

"I'm sorry it happened on the night you're there," she said, "but perhaps it's as well for the parents that it did." She implied: "You'll do everything possible, it matters so much to you." Then she went on with a spurious lightness of tone: "Any news of the Prowler?"

"It looks as if he's having a night off," said Gideon.

Another telephone rang and he glanced toward it—and, while it was still ringing, Kate said, "I can hear that. I'll ring off, darling," and she rang off. He smoothed his chin as he put the receiver back and stretched out for the other.

Kate had done him a world of good; he must find some way of making her understand that.

"Yes," he said, "Gideon here."

"Got a Prowler job," said Whittaker from the Information Room. "Out at Brixton."

This was it; the half-hoped-for and half-feared. Here was the deepest reason for Gideon being at the Yard tonight; here was the greatest challenge. By it, Kate, the kidnapped babies, Matthew, everything and everyone were bundled out of Gideon's mind.

"Bad case?" he barked.

"Usual, I suppose," said Whittaker. "This girl had been out to a youth club. She usually comes home with her boy friend, but the boy had hurt his ankle and couldn't walk so she came back on her own. This swine was crouching just inside the porch of her house; she didn't see him until she was almost on him. He jumped at her and nearly choked the life out of her."

"Anything else?"

"The usual. Cut some of her hair off, but that's all."

"Fetish job," Gideon said, making that half a statement and half a question. "He takes the hair away?"

"Yes."

"Got the color, some of the hair, and . . . ?"

"Chestnut, long wavy, and we've sent a few strands over to the lab."

"Fine," said Gideon. "How is the girl?"

"She'll be all right when she's got over the shock. It happened an hour ago. She wasn't found for twenty minutes or so, and her parents lost their heads. I say she'll be all right," went on Whittaker in a different tone, "and she will be, but he came nearer to choking the life out of her than any of the others. One of these days—"

"I know," said Gideon. "What've we done?"

"The usual. Flashed QR and ST Divisions and all patrol cars, and . . ."

"Wait a minute," Gideon said. "It's a nasty night and we've already one big job on, but we've got to go all out to get the Prowler, too. The two jobs overlap in places. So far they're in the central districts, mostly near the river. I'll call each of the outer ring divisions and get some help. You call available patrol cars and have them block bridges and underground stations. We'll stop buses, too. We want a man with a lock of hair in his pocket, long hairs probably on his clothes. He—"

"You're really going to town," Whittaker broke in. "We can't start searching until—"

"We don't have to search; we only have to threaten to, and our man will panic," said Gideon. "Get a move on—stop all traffic at barriers on bridges, main roads and stations, and put a cordon round."

"There could be hell to pay—"

"There will be if you don't get started," Gideon said. "There won't be many people out tonight, so traffic will be pretty thin. It can be done. Right?"

"You're the boss," said Whittaker. "Right."

"Let me know how things go," said Gideon.

He had been aware of the door opening soon after he'd started to talk, and glanced up to see Appleby, brisk, fresh and rather startled. He put the receiver down but kept his hand on it.

"Hear all that, Charley?"

"Yes. Prowler?"

"Yes. Get on that telephone and call the outer ring Divisions—one for you and one for me, until we've done 'em all. We want a dozen uniformed men from each into QR and ST, quick—and we want our own chaps at the road blocks."

Appleby was already at Lemaitre's desk.

"Then what?"

"We want every pedestrian questioned about a baby seen out tonight, *and* about that hair," said Gideon.

"We need samples of the hair—"

"You may have a lot of trouble in the morning," warned Appleby.

"I'll take what's coming, and if we get the Prowler or those babies we won't have many questions. The fog is all the cover most crooks need; our chaps might as well concentrate on one or two."

"Right," Appleby said.

Both men were on the telephone without respite for twenty minutes. By that time the concentration of police in the Divisions directly concerned was nearly finished, bridge barriers were set up, and the great search was on.

Gideon made written and mental notes as he went on, checked and double-checked, and made sure nothing had been forgotten. If the Prowler and those two children were inside the cordon, they would probably be found.

When it was finished, he lit a cigarette and sat back.

"Anything else doing?" he asked Appleby.

"Not much, yet—only just turned eleven." Appleby smoothed down his brittle-looking, close-cut hair. "Midgeley came on and said he'd told his chaps to lay off the pros tonight; anyone out for business in weather like this deserves a break."

Gideon grunted noncommittally.

"The Hatton Garden chaps are over at Cannon Row," Appleby went on. "Got three at a warehouse in Smithfield, helping themselves to carcasses of mutton. Couple of backdoor jobs in Park Lane. We called off two nightclub raids; wouldn't be likely to get a big enough haul. Had a call from Paris; there's a Johnny on the nine-o'clock plane carrying about two hundred watches—we've tipped off the Customs. That chap Grey over at Cannon Row for the landlady murders has collapsed—he's been sent to the hospital, and old Gore thinks it's genuine."

"Something I needn't worry about now," Gideon said. "And what else?"

"That's about all."

"Enough," said Gideon ruefully.

He had come to get the Prowler, because the Prowler was doing a lot of harm. It was always the devil when one man seemed able to cock a snook at the police for any length of time, and there was a risk that the Prowler would become more violent the longer he stayed free.

Would he kill?

That was an academic question. He would terrify, anyhow. Whittaker could say that his latest victim would be all right, but how did he know? What kind of shock to the nervous system was a thing like this? If it happened to one of his daughters he wouldn't be complacent about it; he—

A telephone rang.

"Gideon," he said.

"There's a Mrs. Penn on the line, sir," said the operator, "and she particularly wants to speak to you."

"Penn?"

"Yes."

"Got her address?"

"Yes, sir, she's at twenty-one Horley Street, Fulham."

"AB Division?"

"That's right, sir."

"Put her through," said Gideon.

Here was the harassed, worried, stubborn and courageous Mrs. Penn, the woman whose young husband had run out on her, and who was sure that something "awful" had happened. He wondered how she had got hold of his name, and wondered also if he could find out more than Lemaitre or the Divisional men had yet been able to discover.

He waited for a long time.

Then the operator came on the line.

"Sorry about that, sir, she's gone off—been cut off, prob'ly. Shall I put her through when she comes on again?"

"Yes," said Gideon, "at once."

There was nothing he could do.

In that part of southwest London covered by the ST and the QR Divisions, the police were not only out in strength, but they were in a much more angry mood than usual, for the Prowler had often struck on the borders of the two Divisions, and the Divisional Superintendents hadn't minced words when they had said what they thought of the men on the beat. That, of course, was unjust. The Criminal Investigation Department was fairly well up to strength, but the uniformed branches were short one man in three of full establishment. The Superintendents knew it, but they also knew that something was needed to get their men right on their toes tonight, and a few nicely chosen words to individuals for passing on through sergeants had that effect. There was more: if the Prowler was caught it would be a feather in the Divisional cap.

Above everything, Gideon was on the rampage.

The fog was not so bad in that part of London, but patchy. The Prowler might decide to call it a day, but the police would assume that he hadn't. Still, facts were facts. In that part of London there were nine times as many streets as there were policemen, and even when the reinforcements arrived there would still be many more streets than policemen. Some of the streets were so long that, even on a clear night, it was difficult to see from one end to the other. The Prowler might lurk in one street for an hour, and not run the slightest risk. He would hide in a doorway, too, or behind hedges or walls—always in the most unexpected place; but he only attacked from the front doors or the gardens of the houses of his victims. Only two certain things were known about him: the shiny face, probably a mask, and the fact that he always knew where to attack. He must study the places where he was going to work, being sure that a young girl lived there.

He usually chose girls in their late 'teens; pretty girls, too.

Jennifer Lewis was nineteen.

She was not usually afraid of the dark or afraid of the Prowler, for the Prowler although familiar as a name, was someone out of a book—a creature one read about but who didn't really exist. She would not have worried about walking home on her own that night, except for the man who had sat on the bus opposite her and kept looking at her, and who had jumped off the bus just after her.

Her home, in Middleton Street, Brixton, was over ten minutes' walk from the bus stop, and part of the way it was along narrow, ill-lit streets. Because of the patchy fog, she couldn't walk quite so quickly tonight; sometimes, near street lamps, it was almost dazzling, at others she found herself on the curb when she thought she was in the middle of the pavement.

She was a pretty girl, with a nice figure and nice legs. Attractive in every way. She had a boy friend whom she felt sure she was going to marry in a few years' time, but he was away on his National Service, and Jennifer Lewis believed that, if your own boy friend couldn't see you home, no boy should.

The man followed her; or she thought he did.

She didn't even see him when she looked round, but she could hear his footsteps, and they always seemed to be exactly the same distance away. She turned two corners, rather slowly each time, and he still came on. By then she was breathing hard and hating her fears, quickening her pace whenever she could, dreading moments when she had to slow down.

Then the footsteps behind her stopped.

She listened for a few seconds, fearful that they would start again, but they didn't. She tried to convince herself that the man had reached his home, that he hadn't been following her, but her imagination began to play tricks, and she was almost sure that he was tiptoeing after her, making no noise. Could he be walking on his stockinged feet?

She strained her ears for the slightest sound, but there was none. The streets were deserted. Lights shone at the front of a few houses, but these were few and far between. The night was clearer as she neared her own street, and at last she came within sight of the lamp and the post box at the corner. For the first time since she had left the bus, she felt relief from tension, although she still walked quickly. As it happened, there was no street light near the front of her home, and, as the family lived at the back, there would be no light at the front windows. She passed the lighted window of one house, several doors away, and saw the shadows of a man and woman against the blind.

Now she walked more naturally, and without tension.

It was very nasty just here, the middle of a thicker fog patch, but there was no longer any danger of losing her way or wandering into the curb, because the gate of her house was painted a pale blue and couldn't be mistaken. She saw it, looking almost as if it were coated with luminous paint, and opened it quickly. It squeaked a little, but she expected that. The silence about her was so complete that, of itself, it seemed frightening.

Yet she was no longer frightened.

She did not think of the Prowler.

The porch of the house was narrow, and normally she could see every inch of it from the gate, but tonight the fog put it out of sight, as well as the door, which was painted black. She took three short steps toward the porch. . . .

A figure appeared in front of her, the figure of a leaping man.

Pain born of fear slashed across her breast; then came horror. But before she could scream, before she even tried to, the man's hands were at her throat. She felt the pressure of his fingers, suddenly and savagely brutal.

Her own arms were free and waving wildly.

She felt herself carried backward by the man's weight, and would have fallen but for his gripping fingers. She couldn't breathe, had no hope at all of shouting, of calling for help. His face was close to hers, a hideous, grinning face, a *mask* of a face.

Then she kicked him.

She wore sensible walking shoes with solid toe caps and felt the kick strike home and heard him wince, even felt him relax his grip. She kicked again with all her strength, and for the second time the toe cap struck home. This time there was a sharp sound; she had caught him squarely on the shin. Again his fingers relaxed but didn't let go altogether. She had time to clutch at his wrists, and dug her fingernails into the flesh.

All the time she saw that leering mask of a face and heard him breathing, felt his hot breath on her cheeks.

She could breathe.

She screamed.

"Help!" she shrieked, and the sound came shrill and louder than she had dared hope. *"Help, help, help!"* She pulled despairingly at the man's wrists, feeling them warm and sticky where blood came from the scratches, and in her terror she kept screaming and kicking and writhing—until suddenly he struck her viciously across the face. She went staggering, gasping as he leaped for her again.

She fell, but her hands were free for a moment and she struck out blindly. She caught her finger under the edge of that grinning mask, and actually dislodged the mask itself; when she struck again it slid off his face but was held by string or elastic in a grotesque position alongside him. He seemed like a two-headed monster—and the bared teeth and the savagery on his real face were worse by far than the false one.

"Heeeeelp!" she screeched into the dark night, but could hear nothing, felt only the fingers of his left hand at her throat again as he knelt on her. She saw something bright and glinting in his other hand.

A *knife*.

Oh, God, no!

Then she felt a tug at her hair. She didn't realize what he was doing, but, as she fought, he banged her head against the cold stone of the ground, and she felt great pain.

She nearly lost consciousness.

Then footsteps sounded; of running men.

The Prowler raised Jennifer's head and banged it down three times, but at the third he peered upward into the murk, as if only then hearing the footsteps. He let her go, and jumped up. Men were coming in the same direction as the girl had come. The Prowler turned in the other as soon as he reached the pavement, and started to run—and his rubber-soled shoes made little sound.

Clearly, a man said, "Hear that?"

"Someone running."

"After him!"

"Never mind him; we want to find who screamed."

They were approaching more slowly now, and the beam of a torch lit up the wreathing fog. The padding footsteps of the Prowler were fading.

A street door opened, and a man appeared with a woman just behind him. The two men were almost level with the doorway.

"What's happening?" asked the man from the house. "We heard . . ."

"Someone screamed," said one of the two men abruptly. "Must have been near here. You look for her; we'll go after the swine who ran away." He started to move quickly, but already the slither of padding footsteps had faded, and not far along Middleton Street there were turnings to the right and left, and not far beyond these, other turnings which led in several different directions.

The men reached the first corner, and hesitated.

The man and woman whose shadows had appeared on the blind of the house near Jennifer's were now walking toward the spot where she lay, while other doors opened, other neighbors appeared and called out.

The first neighbor saw Jennifer lying there, and his wife exclaimed, "Look!" He went to Jennifer quickly, shining the torch—on her legs, both bent, her skirt, which was rucked up, one hand, her face, her chestnut hair, which had come loose from the tight-fitting hat, and:

"Look, that's *blood,*" the woman neighbor gasped.

6

The Con Man

Gideon lifted the receiver of the ringing telephone slowly, and before he put it to his ear he finished reading one of the reports which had just come in from NE Division, which covered part of the East End of London, and part of the riverside area. It did not really say very much, but the little was interesting.

London did not have gangs in the accepted sense, but it housed several gangs which worked all the southern race courses, and they had been very quiet of late. Tonight, said the NE Divisional Report, the two largest, Melky's gang and the Wide boys, were out in strength, and it looked as if there might be a clash. There was no indication yet of the place of meeting, and no certainty that there would be trouble.

The irony was that the Divisional man asked if the Yard could find them additional men.

"Would happen tonight," Gideon grumbled to Appleby, who was reading a copy of the same report, and then he said into the telephone, "Gideon."

Appleby saw the way his great body seemed to gather, as if for a leap, and saw the glint in his eyes.

73

"Where?" he demanded, and wrote swiftly.

"Time?" He made a note.

"I've got it," he said. "You contact the Divisional at once. I'll send photographers, fingerprints and a D.I. Have the place ready for them; we want anything we can get. *Wait*. What color was her hair? . . . Chestnut color and wavy, good—tell the Division to send those scrapings over at once. . . . I don't give a damn how difficult it might be!" he roared. "Get it here! . . . All right."

He rang off.

Appleby looked across, grinning, as if about to make some crack; Gideon's glare stopped him.

"Who've we got in?" Gideon demanded.

"Piper's just back, from a false alarm in Grosvenor Square."

"He'll do." He lifted the receiver again, said, "Ask Mr. Piper to come in at once," and then rang off, but only to pick up another telephone. "Give me Laboratory," he said, and as he waited looked across at Appleby. "Who's on duty up there, do you know?"

"Gibb."

"Thanks, hello . . . Gibb? . . . Gideon . . . Fine, thanks, but busy. Listen: I've got a Prowler job and we want something quick. Girl seems to have scratched his face, and we're sending for scrapings from her fingernails. Have them put through the tests for blood group, will you? We might be glad of it."

"As soon as the scrapings come."

"Thanks," said Gideon warmly. He put down the receiver again, and saw that Appleby was writing with more than his customary speed, as if he was anxious not to do anything wrong. Gideon smothered a grin as Appleby glanced up but didn't speak.

After a moment of almost startling silence there was a tap at the door. Chief Inspector Piper came in, big and fleshy and with florid skin—a man on whom C.I.D. *ex-ranks* seemed to be indelibly stamped. He had rather small, dark blue eyes.

"Hello, Piper," Gideon said. "Got a Prowler lead."

Piper's eyes lit up.

"Putting me on it, sir?"

"Yes."

"Thanks."

"Get two men from Fingerprints, two photographers for an outside job and any sergeant you like to fifty-one Middleton Street, Brixton," Gideon ordered. "A girl named Jennifer Lewis put up a fight. Fingernail scrapings are on their way, but you might pick up a lot more to help."

Gideon paused and Piper looked as if he was bursting to get on his way.

"Anything else, sir?"

"Yes. A papier-mache mask was found near the girl; one of those children's Guy Fawkes things. We've suspected that he wears a mask for some time—either for disguise to frighten his victims even more, or both. That's the lot."

"Thanks," said Piper, and went out twice as quickly as he had come in.

Appleby looked up, smiling openly this time.

"Like offering a kid an ice cream," he said.

"Like offering you a nip," said Gideon, and bent down, opened a cupboard in his desk and took out whisky, a siphon of soda, and two glasses. "Come and get it."

Appleby looked as if he couldn't believe his own eyes, but he got up.

Gideon called the Information Room again, and gave crisp instructions as Appleby, at a motion of Gideon's hand, began to pour out.

"Get moving on this," Gideon ordered, while whisky

was rippling and the instructions poured out of him. "All available men to close in to points within one mile of Brixton Town Hall. The Prowler attacked again near there. Now believed to be wearing a painted Guy Fawkes mask. He tried to kill this time; we don't know whether he's succeeded yet. Anyway, it makes him ten times more dangerous. Warn all women seen alone in the vicinity, make them go in pairs or with male escorts wherever possible. . . . Got all that?"

There was a pause.

"Okay," he grunted, and put down the receiver. When he looked at Appleby it was almost a glare. "The swine will go to earth somewhere inside the cordon, or else he'll find a weak spot and slip through."

"Take it easy," Appleby abjured, almost spilling his whisky. "Not often you take a gloomy view."

"Just struck me that we've already got a hundred men within easy reach of the scene of attack. If we'd had another half hour to work in, we would probably have had the cordon closed before he had a chance to get through it. That looks like Prowler's luck to me." Unexpectedly Gideon grinned, and picked up his drink.

"You're right, though. When you've finished that drink, how about a walk?"

"All right, I'll go down to the Information Room and make sure that everything's being done," Appleby said dryly.

He drank up quickly and went out.

Gideon sipped again, lit another cigarette, and then picked up the telephone; this was one long series of talks and reports, and it wasn't possible to give much concentrated thought to any one thing. That was the Commander's cross; and the cross of the Chief Superintendent on Nights, too. From Superintendents down to detective officers, the men who went out on specific jobs had one thing only on their minds; thus, they could concentrate on it. They had to, or they would never get results. Sitting here like a spider trapped in the middle of his own web, it was almost possible to envy Piper. Gideon could see everything that was happening, every fly they were trying to trap, but he couldn't concentrate. He had to be dispassionate, too, and so could sympathize if the NE Divisional Super cursed the Yard for saying "no" to the request for extra help; to that Superintendent, the fact that the gangs were out was the most important single fact of the night.

"Get me NE Division," Gideon said into the telephone.

"Yes, sir."

Gideon put back the receiver again and glanced through a number of other notes and reports while he waited. The brown-clad sergeant came in, with three short typewritten memoranda from divisions. Gideon made more penciled notes, and wondered whether anything was happening at Lemaitre's home, and how Lem was getting on with Fifi. If there had been any trouble, word of it would surely have come in by now. He wondered about Mrs. Penn; why she had asked for him, and then rung off—or else been cut off but had not troubled to call again.

Why did it nag at him?

She lived in AB Division, and there was plenty doing there. Funny thing he couldn't get her out of his mind.

There was nothing new about the baby hunt. The other two infants were still missing, and the woman Harris in her little kitchen was probably saying exactly the same thing over and over again, still blaming herself; and if her child was killed she would always blame herself for going next door for an hour and leaving it alone, asleep. The sturdy husband of hers

77

probably had exactly the same dazed, almost stupefied look.

It was an hour since Gideon had been told that the first baby had been found dead.

The telephone rang, and his lift of the receiver was automatic.

"Gideon."

"Your call to Mr. Hemmingway of NE Division, sir."

"Yes, put him through." Been a long time coming, he reflected, and began sardonically, "Hello, Hemmy, been having a nice sleep?"

Superintendent Hemmingway was one of the older men in the Divisions, and he preferred to work mostly at night, when his beat was always busier. Like Appleby, he was only a year or two off retirement. Like Appleby, he seemed to have more zest for his job now than when he had first taken over the Division. He didn't mince words, and he was as familiar with his beat as Gideon was with London's Square Mile.

He knew the names, addresses, ages, friends, relatives and habits of the hundreds of small-time and big-time crooks who lived in his division. He knew just which of the stall-holders in the Sunday markets would handle stolen goods knowingly, and those who wouldn't take a chance. He knew when a man was on the run and when one was having a rest. He was reputed to be able to say who had done any job in the division or outside it, from the trade-mark left by the crook, and there were those who said that although fingerprints were not his special subject he could look at a print through the magnifying glass that he always carried and, if it was known to him, identify it almost as quickly as they could in Records. Even allowing for some exaggeration, there was a lot of truth in all of this.

On routine, and on general knowledge as well as

specialized knowledge, Hemmingway was the best man in the Divisions. But he had a weakness, as they all had a weakness, and one of Gideon's difficulties was that of making sure that it did no great harm.

Hemmingway's weakness was that he always took the short view; the long view was something he couldn't see. He lacked not only imagination, but also the ability to look ahead and see what was likely to develop out of a crime or a series of crimes. He could tackle what had happened as well as any man alive, but he lacked the little something extra which would enable him to forestall the crooks' next move.

"Sleep," growled Hemmingway. "How about those men I want, Gee-Gee?"

"Wish I could," said Gideon.

"Talk sense," said Hemmingway, his voice rising. "I've got to have them. There are twenty-five or thirty of the Wide boys out; thing like this doesn't happen more than once a year. Looks as if they're going to mix it. We've got to stop them from clashing."

"Hem, we've got two big jobs on—the baby snatching and the Prowler—and I've called every available man I can from the Divisions. Can't you handle your own boys?"

There was a moment of silence.

Then the door opened, and Gideon looked up and was startled to see Lemaitre come in.

Lemaitre was as pale as he had been earlier in the evening, and his dark eyes were shiny and very bright. His lips were set tightly, and he looked as if he would gladly punch the nose of the first man who got in his way. He let the door slam, which wasn't like him, and stood staring at Gideon, his yellow-and-black tie a little too bright and his shoes too light a brown.

"Look here, George," Hemmingway said at last, and it was obvious that he had been counting ten before speaking; his was not often the way of sweet reason. "You've got those two jobs covered, and if the worst comes to the worst you'll fix 'em in a few days' time. We *live* with the gangs out here. If we can't stop them from fighting tonight, every kid who's got the strength will be thumbing his nose at our coppers for the next couple of months. I want twenty more men than I've got, and that's half the number I really need. Fix it, won't you? Just five carloads—"

"I'll send two," Gideon said abruptly. "We're stretched too far tonight, but I'll send two."

"Listen, George—"

"Be seeing you," said Gideon, and added a mumbling "G'bye" before he put the receiver down. If he'd had his way he would have sent a dozen Squad cars, but far too much was happening. Whatever success they had against the gangs, there would be more trouble later; they were hardy animals. The Prowler and the baby snatcher were much more deadly now.

Lemaitre was still standing there quite still, and his clenched fists were moving slightly, as if he was tensing his fingers all the time.

Gideon took out another glass, poured two fingers, splashing in a little soda, and stood up and carried the drink to Lemaitre. Lemaitre took it, and tossed half of it down, without saying a word.

Time was flying and time was precious, but this was a moment to take things slowly.

"Hello, Lem," Gideon said. "Everything's happening."

"You're telling me," said Lemaitre. "I want something to do outside."

Gideon stared back as he sipped his own drink.

He could let it go at that and send Lemaitre out, with his Fifi troubles burning white hot inside him, or he could try to make Lemaitre talk. Given half an hour, given even a quarter of an hour in which he could be sure of no interruptions, he would probably be able to work on Lemaitre, and help him; but there was no such certainty and Appleby would be back any minute.

"Got two jobs," he said quietly. "Hemmingway's in a flap, Melky's and the Wide boys are out tonight and he thinks they're going to fight it out. He wants three times as many men as we can send him, and my name's mud. If you go, he'll probably think we're really doing everything we can, anyhow."

Lemaitre said flatly, "What's the other job?"

"That Penn woman who's worried about her husband. I want a man to go and see her. She called up again and then rang off before—"

"Women," said Lemaitre, between clenched teeth. "She probably drove him into the Thames. If I had my way—" He broke off, took out a fresh cigarette, lit it from the stub of the one he was smoking, and then moved to squash the stub out on an ashtray. "I'll go over to NE."

"Tell Hemmingway I'll send more men when I can," Gideon said, paused, then added in the same tone of voice, "Of course, the real thing I want from you is an opinion on the situation over there. Hemmingway sees it just from his point of view, the biggest thing they have in the Division. But if you agree that it's really ugly, I'll get more men over there."

"Okay," said Lemaitre.

"What's it like out?" asked Gideon.

"Could be worse—still quicker to travel by car than tube, but it won't be if it gets much thicker," said Lemaitre. "Okay, George, thanks."

"Forget it." Gideon stood up. Appleby still wasn't back and it might be a good moment to speak personally, after all. "What did you run into, Lem?"

The reply came like a bullet.

81

"She's walked out on me."

"Oh, hell!" said Gideon, and for a moment he felt a surge of relief, tinged with understanding. "Sure?"

"Just packed up and walked out, clothes, knick-knacks, everything." Lemaitre found a taut grin. "I know what you're thinking; it will be a good thing in the long run. I might agree with you when I'm used to the idea, but I always thought that in spite of everything, at heart she—"

He broke off.

There was a bright sheen in his eyes, his voice was thick, and he couldn't bring out the words "loved me." He was a man in his forties and men didn't come tougher; yet the wrong note now would have him blubbering.

"Lem," Gideon said.

"Oh, forget it. There's nothing you can say."

"Not so sure," said Gideon. Blessedly, the telephones were silent and there were no footsteps in the passage. "It isn't so long ago that I half expected to get home and find the same situation. Quite sure that the only thing that kept Kate home were the kids. When they were out of the puppy stage I thought she'd go. Instead, we're—well, it's in the past, Lem. This crisis could be the turning point for you, too."

Lemaitre's face was working.

"See what you mean," he said jerkily. "Thanks, George. I'll go and smack a few heads for Hemming-way." He nodded and went out, letting the door slam, and his footsteps sounded loud and clear along the stone passage.

Gideon moved slowly toward his desk and, without sitting down, picked up the telephone. He wanted a lot of time, but had very little; he had to be quick. He called for NE Division again and this time Hemming-way came through almost at once.

"Found me another copper?" he demanded abruptly. The tone of his voice suggested that he hadn't taken umbrage; he was too old a hand.

"Yes," said Gideon. "Hemmy, listen. Lemaitre's coming over. I thought I'd warn you that he's having some domestic trouble and he'd like to break a few bones. If it comes to a fight anywhere, try and get him into it. He'll be worth half a dozen of your chaps, and—"

"Not on your life. My coppers are as good as any who come from the Yard," said Hemmingway. "But I'll nurse him, George."

"Any change with you?"

"Just heard that they seem to be heading for the old Dockside Club and the Red Lion Gymnasium," said Hemmingway, "and if they do we can seal them off, let them fight it out, then nab them for breach of the peace as they come out."

Gideon didn't speak.

"Gone deaf?" asked Hemmingway.

"You did say this was the Melky gang and the Wide boys, didn't you?"

"Yes."

"Shouldn't have thought they would hand themselves to you on a plate," mused Gideon. "You know them better than I do, though."

"When they want to cut one another's throats they forget every bit of common sense they ever had, and it never was very much," said Hemmingway. "There've been rumors of trouble for a long time. The Wide boys have been working the Melky gang's race tracks. When it's like that, it's just a gang war, and all they want is to fight it out. They get like your Soho boys, George!"

"How do my Soho boys get?" asked Gideon dryly.

"So that they almost forget the police exist," said Hemmingway with a chuckle. "They think they can do

83

what they like and get away with it. Take it from me, this is just between the gangs. Okay! I'll put Lemaitre in the front line but distrust his judgment for the night, that about it?"

"Right on the nail," said Gideon.

He put down the receiver, then slowly rounded his desk. He sat for a few seconds staring at the window, where the mist was swirling; it looked as if a wind was moving it. Then he turned back to the desk. There were notes about worried Mrs. Penn, who still hadn't called him again, and there was a note: *"Jennifer Lewis— dead?"* He'd know soon enough, and if she died it would put the Prowler right at the top of the Yard's list of jobs that must be done quickly. As it was, the morning newspapers would be pretty rough, unless the Prowler was caught during the night. There would be the usual questions loaded with innuendo—why hadn't the Prowler been caught long ago, he'd been active quite long enough, and so on. One or two of the newspapers would probably add that it was a scandal that the police were so far below strength, and imply that those who were on the strength weren't up to standard. So far as the Prowler was concerned, there was cause for prodding—he ought to be safe in jail. Was there any way of making sure they got him tonight? To Gideon, that was the most vital job of all.

7

The Night Warms Up

It wasn't long since the cordon had been tightened round the Brixton area, but Gideon was already beginning to feel impatient. If they were going to catch the Prowler, it would probably be done quickly. Every minute he stayed free helped him. In an hour's time, they might as well call the whole thing off. An hour? It was nearly half past eleven and he didn't need reminding that the night had only just started.

Piper was probably just as anxious as he.

He had another worry in his mind, now—about NE and the two big gangs. Hemmingway knew them so well that he was almost certainly right, but the Divisional man had drawn the picture in overtones. The gangs did not ignore the police, and were usually careful to avoid tangling with them; but it looked almost as if they were ready for a tangle tonight. Perhaps they thought that in the fog they could get to their respective headquarters without the police realizing that it was a gathering of opposing forces. Hemmingway had been reasonably well pleased with the two Squad cars, after all; he had probably planned on the assumption that he would get only half what he asked for.

Gideon grinned.

Appleby came back, his footsteps brisk, his manner lively when he entered the office.

"Everything well in hand," he said, "and you've got the Divisions by the tail all right." Obviously he enjoyed saying that. "They'll get the Prowler tonight or bust. You know the kind of thing: Scouts' honor."

"Yes. Nothing in?"

"So far they've questioned about seventy men, none of them with the girl's hair on his coat, or any indication that he's used a mask," said Appleby. "Probably before the night's out we'll have twice the average number of false reports that the Prowler's been seen." He sat at his desk, a little smug and, for the first time, really irritating Gideon; it seemed clear that for some obscure reason he didn't really agree with what had been done. Behind any such attitude there might well be a consciousness that he and the usual Night Superintendent had fallen down on the Prowler, and he would be most glad if Gideon had a failure. The human reaction was the same in policemen as in anyone else. "Two warehouse jobs out at Stepney," he added.

Gideon said abruptly, "Stepney?"

"Yep."

"Where about?"

"Near the river."

"Close to the QR and NE Divisional lines," remarked Gideon. "Big jobs?"

"One lorry load of cigarettes which should have been out of the warehouse at five in the morning, one lorry load of scrap metal."

"They get away?"

"Yep."

"Charley, you have a look at this," said Gideon, and got up and went across to Appleby's desk. They stood together, looking at Gideon's notes. "Hemmingway reports that Melky and the Wide boys gangs are on the move, heading for their headquarters, and I've sent him a couple of Squad cars—Lemaitre wanted something to do, too, so he's gone over. Now we get two warehouse jobs, right on the border of the Division, and we know that one of the favorite jobs of these gangs is shifting lorry loads of stuff that they can sell easily."

"It smells," said Appleby.

"Hemmingway didn't think so."

"Everything over there smells, so he wouldn't notice a little stinkeroo like this," said Appleby, his eyes brightening. "Want me to talk to the other Divisions bordering Hemmingway's, and find out what's on?"

"Yes."

"Right," said Appleby, and if there had been any resentment, even subconscious, it appeared to have faded completely.

Gideon went back to his own desk, pondered for a few minutes, then picked up the telephone. He noticed that Appleby was watching him, almost covertly, as if Appleby meant to study how he worked. Gideon was not conscious of any difference in his approach tonight, but possibly he was more on edge than usual because of the baby kidnappings and the failure to find the kidnapper. The Prowler job wasn't in the same street, was much more of a challenge to the Yard's pride than the baby snatching, but in terms of human misery the baby job won easily.

"Get me AB Division," he told the operator.

"Yes, sir. Just a moment, sir! The Division's on the line now, if you'll hold on a moment."

"I'll hold on."

The wait was longer than Gideon had expected, but that gave him time to think. He was going to tell AB to send a man to see Mrs. Penn, and he couldn't really explain why he felt that was so important. At least it wouldn't do any harm. He knew exactly what it meant, though. He was going to give an order in the guise of a request, and soon a man would leave Divisional HQ for half an hour or so, and go back and make his report—as hundreds of detective officers and higher ranks were doing at this moment. If you took the short view, there were plenty of police, thousands of them, all out tonight, each one watching, waiting and ready— and much more on their toes than usual because he had prodded them.

It was easy to forget the uniformed men and the detective officers, the men who did the chores.

"You're through, sir."

"That you, Ridge?" asked Gideon.

"Hello, George," said Jacob Ridgway, of the AB Division. "Just been talking to the back room about that baby job; wanted to know what you were giving the press."

"Everything."

"That's what they said. No luck yet?"

"No."

"Only child of the people here," said Ridgeway abruptly. "Middle-aged couple, too. Wanted a kid all their lives and now they've got to order the funeral. Get him, George."

Funny, how even the most case-hardened copper could get soft and almost sentimental over a baby job, Gideon reflected.

"We'll try. Ridge, what do you know about that Mrs. Penn and her missing-husband worry?"

"Nothing, except that she's been round here once or twice by day."

"Can you send a man round to Horley Street to have

a word with her? She rang me, but didn't wait to say anything."

"Using your sixth sense?" asked Ridgway and it was almost a jeer. "Okay, I'll send a chap round to talk to her, and if there seems to be anything to worry about I'll call you back. That all?"

"For now, thanks."

"Okay," said Ridgway.

That was about the time that Piper and the Yard specialists reached 51 Middleton Street. Divisional men had already marked off the area and prepared the ground, and had even thought to bring the injured girl's clothes back from the hospital. The parents and a brother were at the hospital and the police had the run of the house.

In ten minutes, Piper was on the radio telephone to Gideon.

"I've checked the hospital for her fingernail scrapings," he said. "They shouldn't be long. Some hair on her coat. I'm sending that over right away. Wavy and chestnut brown places it." Piper was forceful and direct, exactly what Gideon wanted then.

"What else?"

"That mask: a good-quality theatrical one. It didn't come from Woolworth's after all. It should be a good line for the morning," said Piper. "After we've got the prints photographed."

"Man's prints?"

"Yes. Beauties."

"Anything else?"

Piper seemed exultant with his answer.

"Yes, sir! There's a little privet hedge between the approaches to Number fifty-one and next door. Number fifty-three, and in the soil where the hedge is planted there's a heel mark, plain as we could want. Left heel, I think, worn down on the left side with a mark made by a broken heel protector. No doubt about it."

"You'll get photos and then casts just as soon as you can, won't you?" said Gideon.

"You bet I will," Piper promised,

Within five minutes, the radio had carried the news to the men on the bridges and at stations, and the tempo of the watch seemed to quicken everywhere.

It was not Ridgway's man on his way to see the persistent Mrs. Penn, or any of the Yard and Divisional men concentrated about the Brixton area in the hunt for the Prowler, who came upon the next thing which reached Gideon's ear. It was a youthful policeman named Rider, who was on the borders of two of the outer ring divisions, very near the outskirts of the Metropolitan Police district. He was on his own, patrolling a very different kind of beat from anyone in the heart of London, for this was a residential district for the middle-income group. Here, the roads and streets were wide and often winding, the houses were mostly detached and standing in their own small gardens, most of which were beautifully kept. The fog was not very thick, and in some places it was possible to see easily for several hundred yards.

P.C. Rider's beat was one of the most exclusive. The houses he passed were in the high price range, everyone had a garage, some of the families had two cars. Trees grew along the streets as well as in the gardens. Very few lights were on, for here the local authority economized by keeping only one street lamp in four alight during the night, in spite of protests from those people of the neighborhood who had been robbed in the past, and in spite of the strong protests of the police.

*   *   *

P.C. Rider walked more quickly than usual, because of the cold, but he did not consciously skimp any part of his job. His torch light flashed on doorways and windows as he looked for anything that was remotely suspicious, and when he even thought anything was unusual he went to try the door and the window, probably unheard by the people sleeping in the room just above his head. As he turned a corner, he heard a rustle of sound—it must be a cat, it could even be a dog although few dogs were nocturnal wanderers, it might be a cuddling couple or it might be—

Anything.

Rider saw nothing.

A cat, then?

Usually, if you scared a cat, it scampered and jumped, and you heard or noticed something else. By doing a lot of night work, you learned how to notice these things, but now all Rider noticed was the silence which had followed the scuffling sound. So, he played cunning. He did not flash his torch about the houses near the corner, but plodded on, and, a little way from the spot where he had heard the sound, stopped and bent his head, as if he was lighting a cigarette. A policeman who stopped on his rounds to light a cigarette seemed to be the most unsuspicious policeman in the world.

There was still no sound.

There were bushes in the garden of the house where Rider had heard the rustle, and he knew that a man could crouch there out of sight. But if he went back, it would warn any such man. So instead he stood and shone his torch at the window nearer him and, as if he had noticed something unusual, he walked toward it and opened the wooden gate, which made no sound at all. He reached the porch and shone the torch on the keyhole of the front door—and, as he did so, the rustle came again, this time much fainter.

He looked round quickly.

In vague silhouette against the corner lamp, a crouching man wheeled a bicycle out of the garden of the corner house.

Rider jumped into action.

He leaped one low wall, swung along a narrow drive, and reached the street simultaneously with the man with the bicycle, who had difficulty in keeping his machine upright and keeping the gate open.

"Stop a minute!" Rider called, and went running. "Here! I want a word with you."

The cyclist pushed the cycle free, then cocked a leg over it—but he didn't ride off immediately. Rider saw him turn, while on the saddle, and saw his arm drawn back, as if to throw someting. Rider ducked. He heard the sound of the missile making a funny little noise in the air, then heard it crash on the ground behind him. It made the noise of stone on stone; if that had hit him, it would have made a mess of his face.

He blew his whistle and pulled out his truncheon in one and the same movement. The man pushed off from the curb, only a few yards ahead, probably more scared because he had missed but pinning his faith on the bicycle. Rider knew that he had too good a start to be caught by anyone on foot. So the policeman stopped short, slipped the strap of the truncheon off his wrist and hurled the truncheon. He aimed just in front of the cyclist, hoping to strike the handlebars or the man's hands. He didn't know what he struck, but the cyclist wobbled and, wobbling, swung the wheel so that he was at right angles to the rest of the bicycle.

Now Rider had a chance.

He took three long strides while the cyclist was trying to regain his balance, and was within arm's reach when the man fell heavily, the bicycle clattering and the bell giving a single clear ring which seemed to echo for ages. Rider reached the man as he struggled to get up, and promptly put a hammer lock on him.

"Now what's it all about?" he demanded without excitement. "What have you been up to?"

The man didn't speak, but shivered in the tight painful grasp. Lights appeared at several windows, several men who had heard the police whistle looked out, and one came hurrying from across the road. In less than five minutes Rider found that his captive had two thousand pounds' worth of jewels, stolen from the corner house, tucked in his pockets.

It was a long time before Rider began to realize what a stroke of luck he'd had, and how much good this might do him.

"Something's gone right," Appleby called across to Gideon, less than half an hour after the incident. "They've picked up Lefty Winn, out at KI. Redhanded, too, couple of thousand quids' worth of sparklers in his pocket."

"Luck's one word," Gideon said. "How'd they do it?"

"Copper named Rider kept his eyes and ears open."

"Must make sure I have a word with him next time I'm out at KI," said Gideon. He had been along to Fingerprints for a word with the man in charge, for the mask had arrived with a dozen strands of Jennifer Lewis's hair and had only just come back. "Anything new about Jennifer Lewis?"

"No."

"The babies?"

"No. Here's what's come in." Appleby handed Gideon a sheet of paper on which were several short paragraphs in an immaculate hand. Gideon read:

11:31. Two sailors, ages 19 and 20, attacked and

robbed in train at Fenchurch Street, just been paid off, total loss 131 pounds.

11:35. Negative reports from GH and CD on baby hunt.

11:39. Three men sighted breaking into a warehouse in Chelsea, all under charge.

11:41. Negative reports from Information on the Prowler job.

11:49. Smash-and-grab in High Street, Ealing, by two men in an unidentified car. Window smashed, amount of loss not yet known.

11:50. Information Room reports that there have been nineteen reports of the Prowler being seen in eleven different areas.

11:59. Body taken out of the Thames at Rotherhithe by River Police—been immersed several days. Medical report to follow.

12:00. Hit-and-run accident in High Street, Wandsworth, woman of 72 severely injured, now on way to hospital.

Gideon sat back and then heard the booming note of Big Ben. The bell sounded very near, as if it were just outside the window, not a couple of hundred yards away.

"Warming up, eh? Notice anything that isn't there?"

"Sins of the old omission? No," said Appleby. He reached out for the list, frowning a little, showing his white teeth in the set kind of smile, as if he must look on the bright side at all costs. "No," he repeated, "what have you noticed?"

"Almost a complete blank in the East End—no warehouse jobs, no free fights, no drunk beating his wife up. Funny business about the East End tonight; somehow I don't like it. If we don't pick up the Prowler soon I'm going to get more men over to Hemmingway. Can't say he didn't ask for them. I—"

His telephong rang.

"I'll get it," he said, and went across like a great bear, plucking up the receiver and growling, "Gideon."

Appleby saw his expression change, and knew that this news hurt him.

It hurt badly.

"They've just found a second baby," Whittaker said to Gideon. "Suffocated, like the first one, in the garden of an empty house near its home."

"Whereabouts?" Gideon demanded sharply.

"Quinn Street, Chelsea. 'Bout half a mile from the place they found the other one. That's—"

"I know where it is," said Gideon, and went on in the same sharp voice. "One was found about half a mile west of Hurdle Street, the other half a mile east. Close a cordon round the whole area."

"Right," said Whittaker.

Gideon rang off, and Appleby said gruffly, "The Harris kid hasn't much chance now, I bet."

8

Tricks

"Of course he'll be all right, May," said Lucy Fraser. "No one would do any harm to a little baby. You needn't worry; he'll be all right. I'll bet I know what it is, too. Someone has lost a baby and they've stolen yours to try to make up for it. I'm sure you needn't worry. They'll look after it as if it was their own, and the police will soon find them, and everything will be all right."

May Harris looked up at her blankly.

The two husbands were in the front room, talking to one of the policemen; most of the police had gone now, but two were on duty outside, and there were several people in the street, although it was well after midnight, and just here the fog was as thick as it had been at any time during the night.

"I should never have left him" May said drearily. "It was ever so good of you and Jim to want us to see the program, but one of us ought to have stayed behind; if we had, this wouldn't have happened. I'll never forgive myself."

"But he'll be all *right*, May!"

"If he'll be all right, why haven't they found him?" Mrs. Harris asked in a lifeless voice. "It's nearly three hours now, and you'd think every policeman in London was here from the crowd outside."

"Mum," said Jacqueline Harris, who was sitting by her sister's side on the sofa in the kitchen, "I'm sure Mrs. Fraser's right, too; no one would hurt Baby."

"Of course they wouldn't," Millicent said in a scared voice.

They were fifteen-year-old twins, who had come home just before ten o'clock to find the street crowded and to discover with horror that disaster had struck their home. Millicent was fair and fluffy and rather plump. Jacqueline was dark and thin and very much like her mother, although much tidier in appearance. Each wore gym tunics of navy blue, white blouses and long black stockings, and they sat very close together, looking as helpless as they felt, and watching their mother in her blank distress.

For a few moments there was silence. Then Mrs. Harris said sharply:

"What are they in the front room so long for?" She jumped up. "They've been there a long time. What are they saying to Fred?" She rushed into the narrow passage, with Mrs. Fraser after her and the two girls standing up and staring as if they had no idea what to do next; they were pale, they were tired, their eyes were glassy with anxiety and fatigue. This was the first serious emergency in their lives, and they felt so utterly useless.

"If we don't get Baby back, what will Mum *do?*" Jacqueline asked in a whisper.

"Don't even talk about it," Millicent said.

Then they heard their mother burst out as she entered the front room. "What's going on here, what are you so long for? I don't want you to keep anything from me, even if it's the worst." She glanced round at the four men—her husband, Fraser, Willy Smith, the Divisional Night Superintendent, and a sergeant.

Harris looked less stupefied now, as if he was beginnning to feel again. There was a little color in his lips and a spark in his eyes as he moved toward his wife.

"They don't want anything, May, they've just been asking me a few questions. They—"

"Why aren't they out looking for my child?"

"May, they've got to work their own way, and they're trying all they can to help us," said Harris with gentle patience. "It's no use worrying them too much. Did the girls make you that cup of tea?"

"I don't want any tea! I want—"

"You've got to have a cup, and two of those tablets that the doctor—"

"I'm not going to have any tablets from any doctor," his wife shouted at him. "What do you think I am, Fred Harris? Do you think I want to be drugged to sleep while anything might be happening to my own flesh and blood? I don't care if I never go to sleep again, I'll never rest until we've found him, and if we don't—"

"Now come on, Mother," Harris said, in a voice that was suddenly sharp and authoritative. "It's no use carrying on like this; it's time you pulled yourself together. It's all very well behaving like this with me, but what about the girls? Now stop shouting, and come and have a couple of aspirins even if you won't have the sleeping tablets." He took his wife's arm firmly and forced her out of the front room toward the passage, and, as if startled by his firmness, she went without any further protest.

"He'll be all right now he's got on top of himself," Fraser said to Willy Smith.

The Divisional Superintendent looked pale and flabby, even a little vague, and his smile seemed pointless. He watched the husband and wife go out of the room, and was fully aware that the neighbor, Fraser, looked at him impatiently, as if he couldn't understand the lack of results.

"How well do you know this baby?" Smith asked in a very quiet voice which could not be heard outside the room.

Fraser said, "Well enough to know that if they don't get him back—"

"I mean, to look at," Smith said, in the same soft voice, and his eyes were very hard.

Fraser caught his breath. "Have you found—"

"We found a baby wrapped in a blue shawl in Quinn Street, not very far from here."

"Not—dead?"

"Mr. Fraser, do you know the Harrises' child well enough to be able to identify it?" asked Smith. "I don't want to have to make one of them do it. If you don't, then will your wife—"

"I'll know the child," Fraser said abruplty.

"Then will you make an excuse to come with us for ten minutes?"

"No more?"

"We've got it in the car in the next street."

"Aye, I'll come," said Fraser. "No one will miss me. If anyone does you can tell them I've popped next door for five minutes."

"All right. See to that, sergeant."

"Yes, sir."

"Come on, Mr. Fraser," Willy Smith said.

In a good light outside a police car, the child lay wrapped in its shawl, obviously still with death, yet not outwardly harmed, and with no outer evidence of violence. It had a very thin mat of fair hair, and Fraser

100

looked at it only for a moment before he said hoarsely:

"It's not the Harrises' bairn."

"Sure?"

"The Harris bairn had black hair."

"Well, I suppose that's something," Smith said, and didn't add that, while it gave the Harrises a kind of reprieve, it was the sentence of grief on a newly married couple, who had been so happy in their love and with their first-born a few hours ago.

Willy Smith left Fraser outside the door of 27 Hurdle Street, and then drove off. The child's body was on the way to the morgue, and Smith was glad that he didn't have to take the news to the parents. After a few minutes he told his driver to slow down, and then picked up the radio telephone. He called the Yard, and was asked to hold on; Gideon was on the telephone. Smith sat waiting as his driver edged slowly through the fog, and there was rather an empty look on his face.

Then Gideon came on. "Hello, Willy."

"Hello, George. Thought you'd want to know that the baby found in Quinn Street wasn't the Harrises', so it's the one from Wragg's Division. I've left it to you to tell Wragg."

"All right."

"I'm going back to the Registrar's office now," said Smith. "Nothing likely at Fulham, but two men are still at the Chelsea office; they might get a line. It's worth calling on all parents who've lost a child lately. I'll call you from Chelsea."

"Thanks," said Gideon.

"Didn't realize until tonight how many people get born and how many die in a few weeks," said Smith. "I had a twelve months' coverage done on the job; thought that if the loss of a baby had turned someone's mind it might have taken more than a few days."

"Could do, too," said Gideon. "Fine, thanks."

"Having a nice night?"

"Short of good coppers, that's all," said Gideon, and rang off.

Smith chuckled as he put back his receiver, and then switched off. His driver glanced at him but Smith didn't make any comment. Soon, they pulled up outside the office of the Registrar of Births and Deaths, where a uniformed policeman was on duty, as if those inside needed protection. Smith bustled out of his car and past the man, nodding, and then into the offices. A light shone from the first-floor landing, and Willy Smith went up, not too quickly, for he was a man who lost his breath very easily. He saw moving shadows, and, as he reached the doorway, the elderly, gray-haired Registrar and one of the Divisional men looked up.

"How you doing?" asked Smith.

"Fifteen infants died here last month," said his sergeant. "There was a nasty gastroenteritis epidemic." Smith remembered that as the man spoke. "Nineteen for the rest of the year ending this month."

"Thirty-four in all," Smith said, almost to himself. "Thirty-four." He felt the gaze of the other two men on him as he spoke, but he made no further comment except to thank the Registrar, and ask his man, "Got the list?"

"Yes."

"Good, let's go." Going downstairs was a different matter from walking upstairs, and he hurried and was only slightly out of breath when he reached his car. He slid into his seat and called the Yard again, asked for Gideon, and was put through at once. Gideon's voice was deep and it sounded unflurried, like that of a man whom nothing could really disturb. That was perhaps Gideon's greatest strength, the confidence which he could put into other men.

"What have you got now, Willy?"

"Thirty-four babies within the age group we're after, and that's a hell of a lot to try to tackle tonight," Smith said. "I'd been banking on three or four at the most."

Gideon said, "Hmm."

"Want me to go ahead?"

"Willy," said Gideon quietly, "have another go at the Registrar, and blame me for it. Each death certificate will have the certifying doctor's name, and we'd better check the doctors. Find out from them if they know of any of the bereaved mothers—or fathers, if it comes to that—who went a bit queer. That might give you a lead to two or three names, without making it a major job."

"Good idea," said Smith. "Why don't I get one myself sometimes? Got the Prowler yet?"

"No," said Gideon.

"How's that girl he bashed about?"

"Touch and go," said Gideon.

It was certainly touch and go, and Whittaker had been too optimistic.

Jennifer Lewis was on the operating table at a London hospital, with the night staff and the night-duty surgeon ready to operate, for X-ray photographs had shown a splinter of skull so dangerously lodged that unless it was quickly removed it would almost certainly pierce the brain.

At the hospital, her mother and father and brother waited.

At bridges, stations, bus terminals and other vantage points the police still watched and waited, too, but now the traffic had dwindled to a trickle; there was not work enough for so many men. They could go back to their own Divisions, and some could be sent to Hemmingway; Gideon had only to say the word. He didn't. He told himself that he would wait until half past one before giving up hope of catching the Prowler.

He went up to the laboratory, as much to see what else was going on as to check on the hair and fingernail scrapings. Up here, in the big, airy laboratory, it seemed a different world. Things might be in a hurry, yet everyone moved slowly and almost casually. Two Bunsen burners hissed, one of them with a small white crucible over it. A burette seemed to be blowing bubbles. Gibb, the night chief, was a tall, spindly individual with a pointed chin and rather sour look which experience of him belied. He was peering at a slide on a microscope, and as Gideon came up, he said:

"These are the nail scrapings."

"Anything?"

"Blood."

Gibb laughed. "You guess! I'll tell you as soon as I can. The hair's dark chestnut brown, very healthy, naturally as straight as mine—she probably waves it herself."

"Thanks. So she scratched him for certain."

"I'm talking to the Commander, aren't I?" asked Gibb dryly. "Not a rookie. She could have scratched a pimple off the end of her nose. Okay, okay, probably she didn't."

"Corrected." Gideon said. "What are you cooking?"

"Sudden death by some gastric trouble this afternoon; we're testing for arsenic. Got the body of the woman taken out of the Thames coming up; that'll keep us busy. That arm they fished out of the Thames last week had been in the water three weeks, I would say. There was some green paint sent up, from the shoe of the woman run down in Wandsworth. We've analyzed it but I wouldn't like to name the manufacturer until there've been some further tests. Okay?"

"Let me know when you've finished; I'll send some work up," said Gideon.

He kept a straight face as he left.

In a smaller room nearby, two men were busy making duplicates of a plaster cast which had already arrived from Middleton Street. Piper worked as if he moved on wheels. Gideon inspected the imprint of the heel and the clear indentation of the broken heel protector, and felt a curious tension, a sense of excitement, a feeling that at last the Prowler's days were numbered.

He went down to Records, where the little man with Pince-nez was standing at a desk with fingerprint sheets in his hand.

"Hello, Syd," Gideon said. "Any luck with those prints that Piper sent in?"

"We haven't got 'em on the file, so he's a brand-new criminal for you," said the Records man, as if absently. "I can give you all the dope in ten minutes. It's a tented arch pattern, with a double . . ."

"Thanks," Gideon said, five minutes later, and went down to his office, where Appleby gave the impression that he had just finished the greatest clowning act of his career, he was grinning so broadly. He didn't pass on his joke, and Gideon went to sit down.

It was nearly one when the telephone rang again, and with an automatic movement Gideon lifted it off its cradle and gave his name. Appleby, wreathed in cigarette smoke, was working at one of his minute-by-minute lists.

"Ridgway here," said the AB Divisional man. "Sorry I'm late with this. I thought it had been passed on. The Penn woman. She lives at Horley Street with her mother, but hasn't been home this evening—that's unusual. I checked the house where she lived with her husband. Mrs. Penn left the flat the early part of last month, a few weeks after the husband vanished. Hadn't paid her rent, so she was thrown out. The landlord's a so-and-so. My chap probed a bit, but didn't get anywhere. Can it wait until morning?"

"Oh, God," Gideon groaned. "If she hasn't been home, she might have decided to throw herself into the river, or—" He paused, knowing that he was being unduly gloomy and that, with all the bridges manned, there was a closer watch than usual on the river. Why did he want to dramatize Mrs. Penn, anyhow? "Yes, leave it," he said. "Thanks. Much doing your way?"

"Bit quieter than usual if it weren't for the two main jobs. Before you go," went on Ridgway, "I forgot to tell you earlier that Bigamy Bill's back in town."

Gideon said sharply, "Sure?"

"One of my chaps was at the Roxy Hotel—it's his son's twenty-first birthday tonight—and he called up and said B.B. was there."

"Alone?"

"With a blonde."

"Young?"

"His usual style, bit bosomy but easy on the eye," said Ridgway. "It would be a kindly thing to whisper a word of warning in her ear."

"I'll see what I can do," said Gideon. "Thanks."

"Pleasure," Ridgway said, and rang off.

9

Hope

In the background at the Roxy there was soft music, and, about the room, soft lights. Only a dozen couples were left in the night club, which was in a basement of the hotel, and three of these were elderly tourists, sitting it out on the edge of the tiny dance floor. The *decor* was African, with futuristic drawings of animals and Africans, assegais and tom-toms, and the music, though soft, had a tom-tom-like rhythm given by a dreamy-looking colored man who was playing the drums.

Two of the people on the dance floor were dancing cheek to cheek, the girl in her early twenties with fine, wavy, fair hair and a fair complexion, flushed just then with too much to drink. Her eyes had a glazed look, but she had complete control of her movements, and danced rhythmically. She was plump but nicely built. The man was half a head taller, dark, with receding hair and very fine features. He held her tightly and danced dreamily, and the music seemed never to stop.

But it stopped at last.

The man slid out of the girl's embrace, then twined his arm round her waist again, and they walked together to a table in the corner.

". . . years," the man said in a whispering voice. "Been waiting years for you, Florence, that's the sober truth. I've been waiting for years."

"Oh, *Bill,*" she said.

"Know what I want to do?" Bill asked, nuzzling her white shoulder. "I want to get married. Soon. *Tomorrow.*"

". . . Bill," she sighed.

"Can't *get* married tomorrow," Bill said in a sad voice, "but in a day or two we can." He covered her right hand with his, and the hard surface of a beautiful diamond ring scratched the soft skin of his fingers. "Can't do without you," he went on, "just can't wait."

". . . . *Dar*ling," she cooed.

"Why don't we—" Bill leaned close to her, and finished the sentence so close to her ear that no one else could possibly hear it. Three couples got up and went out, the women yawning. A Polish waiter yawned, too. Business was bad, tips were bad; if they could get rid of the couple in the corner necking, the rest would probably go. The band began to play again, but no more briskly, West Indian music in that African setting.

". . . s'go," breathed Bill.

He stood up, and the girl Florence put her hands in his and let him pull her to her feet. She swayed, apparently very drunk. The diamonds on her finger scintillated so brilliantly that one of the remaining women stared enviously, then plucked at her husband's coat to make sure that he didn't miss this evidence of some man's readiness to spend freely on his love.

Ten minutes later the couple went out into the misty night; the West End was still remarkably clear of fog. The blonde leaned heavily on Bill's arm as they waited for a taxi, which wasn't long in coming.

"Ensor Street," Bill ordered, naming a small street in Soho, and then he helped the blonde in, and climbed in beside her, close beside her.

The taxi vanished about five minutes before a police car pulled up, and a plain-clothes man got out and nodded to the commissionaire as he hurried down to the night club. He looked round, grimaced in disappointment, and then spoke to the head waiter. . . .

"Yes, sir, there was a man like that, and a young lady, but—they go, not long ago, they go."

The Yard man reported by telephone.

"Well, we can't do anything about it," Gideon said gruffly. "No crime to take a girl to your flat even if you've done it fifty times before in—" he broke off. "All right, you come back, nip over to the Grand Hotel, and look slippy. Fingerprints and Photography have someone on the way. Couple of bedrooms have been entered and it looks as if there's a lot of loot. The job was discovered ten minutes ago; there's just a chance you'll be in time to pick up the chap with the stuff on him."

Nine rooms had been broken into at the hotel, and a rough estimate of the valuables stolen was ten thousand pounds.

In spite of concentrated work of all the Departments, the police didn't find a single significant clue.

Gideon replaced the receiver after one thirty, made a note about the Grand Hotel job, then leaned back and stretched—his arms were so long that he looked like a massive birdman. He yawned, then ran his hands through his hair.

"You young chaps," scoffed Appleby, "you can't

109

take it half as well as we old men. Why don't you go and take a nap? I'll call you if anything blows its top."

"Not a bad idea," said Gideon mildly.

"Did we stop Bigamy Bill?"

"Missed him by minutes."

"That son of a gun has all the luck," said Appleby, as if with envy. "Only has to snap his fingers at a girl and she's ready to pop into bed with him, and after that he sells her the marriage idea so well she can't make over her cash and securities fast enough. You know, Gee-Gee," went on Appleby, leaning back in his chair and spreading his hands in the desk, and for once apparently wholly earnest, "human nature beats me. It does, really. Especially girls where a chap like B.B. is concerned. They read about it in the newspapers—once a week or so there's a big spread showing how a crook like Bill got away with it—they get all the juicy details in the *News of the World* and a hell of a lot of awful warnings from judges and magistrates all over the country, and what do they do? Fall for the first charmer they meet. Got any theories about it?" In fact Appleby was not interested in Gideon's theories, only in his own simple Philosophy. "Look at the number of sweeties Bill's fixed, in more ways than one, too. He must be fifty-five if he's a day. I can remember when we had him in dock *for* bigamy. He got six months, but he also got wise to the situation—he could go to any length short of marriage, and get away with it. Since then he must have ruined thirty or forty kids and probably a hell of a lot more we know nothing about, because the poor sinners don't want to tell the world what fools they were and how much he sucked them for. You want to know what I think, Gee-Gee?"

"Yes." This new slant on Appleby interested Gideon; each man had his pet ideas, and some were worth sharing.

110

"We laugh at Bigamy Bill," went on Appleby. "You've only got to mention his name, and you get a grin. Why the first time I heard it tonight I was grinning like a Cheshire cat—half wishing him luck too. You try it tomorrow. Just slip B.B. into the conversation with anyone, and see what happens. Always good for a horse laugh, like stories about ma-in-law and flatfoots on the beat. But the truth is he does a hell of a lot more harm than a chap like the Prowler. You may say I'm talking through my titfertat, but you could be wrong about that. Take the Prowler, now. We're bound to get him soon, or else scare him into being quiet, and at the most he'll have attacked a dozen girls and frightened the wits out of them. Maybe his Lewis girl will pop off, so he'll become a murderer. But B.B. now—he's ruined more girls than the Prowler's ever thought of, and all we can do is to try and warn each new girl before she's swallowed the bait. We've tried to get him on intent to defraud, and what happens? His counsel puts the girl up in the box, and before it's over she admits that she knew exactly what she was doing, and B.B. gets off and laughs at us. Now *there's* a man I'd like to put inside for the rest of his natural."

Appleby stopped, put his head on one side, then ran the length of his forefinger underneath his nose and sniffed with a noise like a distant bandsaw. "Hark at me. Always ought to have worn my collar the wrong way round, and no one ever realized it!"

Gideon said quietly, "There's a lot in it, Charley. The chap who first said the law was an ass had something."

"But it's the law and we're here to enforce it," said Appleby, wrinkling up his face in a rueful grin. "I know, I know, and I can see you're in training for the next Assistant Commissioner. That's the kind of ropey stuff he trots out when he gets a chance. I—"

One of his telephones rang.

"About time someone stopped me gassing," he remarked. "All aboard for the crime stakes; wonder what we've got this time? Anything from rape to murder and dear Mr. Policeman my pussycat's not come 'ome. . . . Appleby speaking."

A telephone rang on Gideon's desk.

"Gideon . . ."

Gideon pushed a note pad away from him as the operator said, "It's Superintendent Smith, sir." He felt himself tense. By now Willy Smith had probably finished his rounds of the doctors who had signed the death certificates of the infants.

"George?"

"Yes, Willy?"

"Got two possibles," Smith said, and there was a note of excitement in his voice. "There's a Mrs. Golightly across the road, at forty-two Hurdle Street; lost her baby about two months ago, and she hadn't been right in the head since. The landlady of the place where she used to live had a baby a few months older, and this Mrs. Golightly used to take it out of its pram up to her own rooms. The landlady gave the Golightlys notice. We got this from a neighbor who knew her before she came to live in Hurdle Street—neighbor's only just heard about the missing Harris baby. That's the most likely. Then there's an unmarried girl whose baby was taken away from her and put into an adoption home a month or two ago. The girl signed the release at her mother's insistence, but ever since she's been a bit queer. She lives at Hill Street, Chelsea."

"That's nearer you than Hurdle Street," Gideon said crisply. "Go and check on her."

"Who'll do Hurdle Street?"

"I will."

"Right," said Willy. "I can get to my place as quick as

112

any patrol car."

He rang off, and Gideon stood up abruptly. Appleby was scribbling a note and looking across at him as if he didn't like his expression.

"What's up?"

"Might be on the track of that baby-snatcher," Gideon said. "I'm going to Hurdle Street. Tell Info to have a patrol car at Number forty-two, quick—No," he changed his mind as he reached the door. "There's a car round the corner from Hurdle Street; have the crew call at Number forty-two—a Mrs. Golightly."

"Gorblimey Golightly!" Appleby exclaimed. "Here's a chance to throw some weight about."

The door closed on his last word, and Gideon almost ran down the corridor.

The fog, thick but on the move in Parliament Square and on the Embankment, was much thinner a little way from the river, and at no time was Gideon slowed down to a crawl. The city was empty and it seemed dead. There was no sound from the river, and no lights showed across from the other side, not even the lights of Battersea Power Station, with its huge chimneys and its massive square block. Now and again another car came toward him, lights ghostly in the murk. There were few policemen about; too few.

He kept picturing Mrs. Harris' face when he had first given her hope and then snatched it away again, and was grimly aware of a kind of personal responsibility which everyone else would scoff at, but which was deep and immovable in him. He could keep in touch with the Information Room and Appleby from the car; there was no need for him to sit at his desk all the time.

He kept the radio on.

There was a cacophony of words and phrases continually spilling into the car as instructions flew to and from the Yard, to and from the Divisions. The dead night seemed to come back to life. There was no light but that of Gideon's headlamps, dipped toward the curbs, but the night seemed full of light—brightly lit offices, houses, clubs, hospitals, homes, police stations. With the radio off it was a dead or at best a sleeping city; with it on there was a pulsing throb of life, of bustling activity, a sense of swift exciting movement everywhere.

Then:

"Calling Commander Gideon, calling Commander Gideon."

"Gideon here," Gideon said. "I can hear you."

"Message from Chief Inspector Lemaitre, sir."

"Let's have it."

"Good reason to believe Mr. Hemmingway right about the situation in NE Division, sir."

"Right. Give me Mr. Appleby."

"Yes, sir."

So Hemmingway had been right and he had been wrong; there seemed nothing particularly sinister about the gathering of gangs in the East End. Well, it wasn't the first time by a long way that he had been wrong. He wished Appleby would hurry, but the man was probably on the telephone, making his cracks, or writing down his notes in that immaculate handwriting, being bright and breezy and hiding—what? Theories about the almost criminal idiocy of the law?

In five minutes, Gideon would be in Hurdle Street.

"Appleby speaking, Commander."

"Charley, listen," said Gideon. "Take half the men we moved into the central districts for the Prowler, and have them go to NE at Hemmingway's disposal. Get 'em there quick."

"Okey dokey."

114

"Thanks," said Gideon.

"Don't run away," said Appleby hastily. "Something else here you ought to know about. Just had a telegram from the *Sureté Nationale*." His pronunciation of that was almost perfect, Gideon noted with surprise; his French accent on that word at least was better than his English. "You know that Guthrie girl who was cut up and buried in the French Pyrenees last year?"

"Yes."

"They've dug up evidence suggesting that there was an Englishman named Forrester with her," said Appleby, "and they say Forrester's on the way from Paris by air—he got away before the Paris people could arrest him. Will we meet him at London's airport?"

"Any evidence?"

"They say they've a basketful, but didn't quote it; they've a man coming over on the same plane to see us. The silly mugs saved a couple of hundred francs by telegraphing instead of getting us on the buzzer, and the aircraft's due in any minute. It's a special flight and had a few spare seats."

"Have the Customs detain Forrester and the Frenchman," said Gideon.

"That's a relief," said Appleby, "I have."

Gideon was surprised into a chuckle.

Appleby rang off, and now Gideon switched off his radio, for he was very near Hurdle Street and didn't want another interruption. He found that his heart was thumping with a most unprofessional anxiety as he turned into Hurdle Street. Where before there had been a crowd not far short of a mob, there were now only one or two people standing about, and a solitary police car. Lights showed at three places, one of them Number 27; that was at the second floor, so Harris had persuaded his wife to go upstairs. The other lights were at the front door and the second-floor window of

115

Number 42—or what he guessed was Number 42.

A Mrs. Golightly had lost her child and had tried to find some solace in another woman's. The landlady must have been seriously worried to have made her leave. It was at least possible—

"Remember the motorcyclist said a *man* was seen carrying the kid," Gideon said to himself almost roughly, as if he resented the way his tension was rising.

He pulled up. Yes, this was Number 42; the black numerals showed on the fanlight. Outside the house a uniformed policeman waited, advancing as Gideon got out of his car. The night was quiet and the fog almost clear here; just a murkiness which gathered about the lights. There was a gentle but rather cold wind stirring what was left of the fog.

"Gideon," said Gideon. "Anything doing here?"

"Been a bit of shouting since the detectives went in sir, but my orders were to stay right here."

"Shouting?" Gideon moved swiftly, with that pulsing, almost frightening beat of heart. Inside this house was exactly the same as the Harrises' across the road. There was a narrow passage, the narrow staircase and at the foot of it an elderly couple who looked scared, dressed in overcoats and night clothes, the woman with gray hair in big curlers, the man nearly bald. With them was a plain-clothes man, saying patiently:

"I am a police officer, and all I want is the answer to a few questions." He recognized Gideon, and moved aside quickly. "Evening, sir."

"Anything?"

"Found a baby upstairs, sir," the man reported. "An ambulance is on the way. Don't know whether we've saved it or not. Half suffocated."

As he spoke, a woman screamed upstairs.

Upon the scream, an ambulance bell rang clearly in the street.

10

Rescue

"Go across to number twenty-nine and ask Mr. or Mrs. Fraser to come over here at once," Gideon said to the man. "Don't let them waste any time." He squeezed past to the stairs, but found time and opportunity to glance at the old couple and to smile with heartening reassurance. "We'll need to know how often Mrs. Golightly has been out tonight," he said. "Is Mr. Golightly up there with her?"

The woman answered, "No, he's away during the week."

Oh, God, thought Gideon.

He hurried up a staircase so narrow that one arm brushed the wall, the other the banisters. The woman upstairs was screaming wildly, a man was speaking— then suddenly the man spoke more sharply; there was a louder scream. Next there came a sharp sound, as of a slap across the face. The ambulance bell had stopped ringing but the beat of the engine suggested that it was now pulling up outside.

Gideon reached the landing.

A bedroom door stood wide open, just beyond the

landing. Two policemen in plain clothes were there, one standing close to an attractive young woman in blue slacks and a tight-fitting gray jersey. She had one hand at her cheek, as if she couldn't believe that she had been struck. Her eyes held a glitter which Gideon had seen too often before—the glitter which suggested that she wasn't sane.

As Gideon drew near, he saw the bed, another policeman kneeling in front of an infant on the bed and applying artificial respiration with enormous hands which looked large enough to break the baby into little pieces.

There was no sign of life in the child.

The pretty woman suddenly snatched her hand away from her face and flew at the man who had struck her, and so great was her fury and so wild her strength that she carried him back toward the wall. Then she turned and ran toward the door, as if she had not noticed Gideon in the way. Her lips were parted as though she were screaming but could not make a sound.

She saw Gideon.

She flung herself at him bodily, as if believing that she could force him back, but, although he couldn't stop a collision, he hardly budged, and she was flattened against him for a moment. Then she struck at him. He caught first one wrist and then the other, and held them tightly in his big fingers, making her helpless although she kicked wildly, stubbing her toes and hurting herself much more than she hurt him.

"Handcuffs," Gideon said sharply.

"Yes, sir." The man she had pushed aside slipped shiny handcuffs out of his pocket as if by sleight of hand and fastened one loop over Mrs. Golightly's wrist, one over his own. Perhaps it was the touch of cold steel, perhaps it was Gideon's massive figure; certainly something quieted her, and she turned away and

118

covered her face with her free hand.

Behind the door were an old raincoat and a faded trilby. Wearing those and the slacks, it was easy to see how she had been taken for a man. Gideon looked at her without compassion.

The ambulance men and a young doctor came in from the landing, and the child lay there, still as death, with those great hands ceaseless in their desperate work of rescue.

Two minutes later, Fraser hurried in, shivering in an overcoat over striped blue pajamas, sparse hair standing on end, eyes watering. The doctor had taken over, saying simply that they must deal with the child here; the ambulance men had gone down to their ambulance for the portable oxygen unit.

"Sorry about this, Mr. Fraser," Gideon said, "but is this the Harris baby?"

Fraser took one look.

"Aye," he said, and everything but dread faded from his eyes. "Aye, don't say—"

He couldn't finish.

"I should say it's fifty-fifty," said Gideon, but in truth he had no idea whether the child had any chance at all. He did not seem able to keep his mind detached about this case, which seemed to be built upon unending tragedy. For there was no doubt that Mrs. Golightly had killed the other two children, no doubt that she should never have been allowed to move about freely until the doctors had made sure of the soundness of her mind.

Her husband knew how she had behaved before, he must have known that she wasn't normal, and yet he had left her alone.

What made men do such crazy, criminal things?

Criminal?

It wasn't legally criminal; just a moral crime.

119

Appleby could say plenty about that. Whatever the reasons, Golightly had left his sick wife alone for days on end, making no arrangement for her to have company. As a result two babies were dead, and one might die, and two mothers might suffer a shock so great that the balance of their minds would be affected just as much as Mrs. Golightly's.

There was another instance of Appleby's example of Bigamy Bill. The greatest crimes could be committed *within* the law. This woman had cunning, she had killed, she would be put into an asylum at "Her Majesty's Pleasure." Her husband had committed the sin of omission. Funny to be quoting and moralizing like Appleby.

Now there was the woman herself to deal with.

Mrs. Golightly was on her way to Scotland Yard, where a doctor was waiting for her; she would be given a sedative and put to bed in Cannon Row, the police station just across the courtyard, and in the morning she would probably wake up quite sane, but aware of what she had done and filled with new despair.

The doctor looked up from the child, only twenty minutes after Gideon had arrived, and brushed his hair back from his damp forehead. Willy Smith had arrived; more policemen were here, as well as a nurse for the child. Gideon saw the way each man stared at the doctor, and realized that he had not been the only policeman who had felt the night's sickening fear.

"He'll be all right," the doctor said.

No one spoke for several seconds, but all stared at the baby inside the plastic oxygen hood, its head on its side, looking peacefully asleep, and with a faint movement at its chest.

"Sure?" grunted Gideon.

"Quite sure."

"Can we tell the parents?"

"Yes."

"Good enough," said Gideon, and nodded to Willy Smith. "Thanks. Come on." He led the way downstairs and into the cold street, and felt as if the only thing in the world that mattered had happened now; that there was cause for supreme contentment, for easing unbearable tension.

Fraser was standing just inside the front doorway of his house, and his wife was behind him, bundled up in a dressing gown.

"Excuse me, sir—"

"The child will be all right," Gideon said quietly, and heard Mrs. Fraser's cry, "Thank *God,*" and then heard her begin to sob.

Soon, he was upstairs at Number 27, where Mrs. Harris was still fully clad but, persuaded by her husband, had lain down on the double bed.

She didn't speak when Gideon told her, but so radiant was her face that Gideon believed he would carry the sight of it in his mind until his dying day, as he would the look of delight, so near elation, on the father's face.

Two babies had died that night, but theirs had been saved. They might feel compassion but they could not share the grief or the hurt.

Willy Smith and Gideon stood by the side of Gideon's car, and a gust of wind came along the street, making Smith clutch at his hat, and causing Gideon to shiver. For the first time, they could now see the outline of every house in the street, and the fog eddied about as

121

if it were anxious to get away as soon as it could.

"Now all you want is the Prowler," Smith said, "but it doesn't look like our night for him, does it?"

"Still time, I suppose," said Gideon. "Did you hear that I'd moved men into NE? The Wide boys and Melky's gang look as if they're spoiling for a fight."

"I heard. Taking their time, aren't they?" Smith shrugged. "I hope they cut themselves to pieces." He paused, but obviously hadn't finished. "I know what I've been meaning to ask you for weeks, George—nothing to do with shop, but about my daughter, Peggy. You know her; she danced a lot with your boy Matthew at that teen-age dance they ran out at the Sports Club in the summer."

"Pretty kid," said Gideon, remembering well. "Must have taken after her mother."

"I helped," Smith grinned. "Don't know whether I ever mentioned it, but she's quite handy with the violin. Not in the top flight like your Pru, but not bad for an amateur, and she's as keen as mustard. I wondered if Pru would give her a few tips, help her to find out if it's worthwhile taking up lessons and going in for it seriously. I shouldn't think it is," added Smith, with an airy nonchalance which didn't deceive Gideon for a moment, "but if she could find out, it would put her out of her misery."

"Shouldn't think Pru would like to sit in judgment," Gideon said. "She doesn't take after her father. But *if* she can help I know she will. I'll tell you what. Sunday afternoons or evenings, when she's not playing with the orchestra or at the BBC studios, we usually have a kind of musical evening at home. Kate plays the piano a bit and—"

"Dad sings," put in Smith.

"Not on your life. One verse of 'Old Man River' is my limit these days. But next time Pru's going to be in, I'll call you and suggest you come over for an hour or two. Have your youngest bring her violin, and let's see what goes on from there."

"First rate," said Smith. "Thanks, Gee-Gee. Now I've got you for a minute, there's another thing, too. You know I run a series of lectures over at Divisional headquarters once a fortnight. General police routine and special subjects, particularly anything that will help to make them think there's some fun in it. We get too many resignations from the chaps who come in full of enthusiasm, find it a bore and resign in their first year," Smith went on. "This is my way to try and get 'em to stay. I've always found out that if you can hold 'em for three years you've got 'em for keeps."

"S'right," agreed Gideon.

"Well, you won't believe it, and I did my damnedest to kill the idea, but a lot of the chaps seem to think that George Gideon is the Big Cheese. Would you—"

Gideon chuckled, a deep, pleased laugh, for that had come so unexpectedly and yet with such obvious sincerity.

"Yes, I'll come and talk to 'em," he said. "Any time you like, within reason."

"I'll fix it soon," Smith said. "Thanks, George. Well, it's time I went to see how crime's getting on in CD Division; been quietish except for that baby job until now. Hell of a relief that's over."

"I know how you feel," said Gideon.

Smith went off. Gideon got into his car, watched by the only two uniformed police who were now in the street. He didn't start the engine immediately, but adjusted his coat and told himself that he seemed to be taking up more room these days, because the car wasn't shrinking. He hadn't been on the scales for months. He flicked the radio to life, and the medley of London's night sprang into the car: odd phrases, odd words and,

123

unexpectedly, a background of dance music. One of the Squad cars was probably near a place where music was being played, but at this hour it seemed odd.

He called Appleby.

"How are things, Charley?"

"You're a fine one," Appleby said. "First time tonight I get a chance of forty winks and you have to wake me up. Things have gone quiet, everywhere a deathly 'ush. If you really want the details—"

"Not if there's nothing big. I thought I'd drive over and see Hemmingway while I'm out."

"I'll hold the fort," Appleby promised. "That plane from Paris arrived, the French chap is on his way, should be here inside the hour. Still foggy out at Hounslow and the Great West Road, but not so bad."

"If the Paris chap really seems to have anything, have the airport police ask Forrester to come to the Yard with them for questions," Gideon said. "If you don't think it's strong enough, let him go and have him tagged."

"Oke."

Gideon hesitated, reluctant to put the receiver down until he knew for certain that there was no news in about the Prowler, but knowing that Appleby would have passed anything so important. The hiatus lasted only a second or two, but he was very conscious of it; then he asked almost too quickly:

"How's the Lewis girl?"

"Nothing new," said Appleby. "Piper's back; he did quite a job. The mask will be trotted round to London suppliers in the morning, telephotos of the heel print will go out tonight. If you ask me, you could take everyone off the cordon now. We're not going to get Mr. P. tonight."

"You could be right," conceded Gideon. "Give 'em a bit longer—if he's still out he won't be able to hide all night, so we might catch him yet."

"You're a sticker, you are," Appleby said, and then suddenly burst out laughing. "Stickier than glue. Three G's for you in future, Gee-Gee!" Still tickled by his wit, he rang off, and Gideon flicked the radio off ruefully. Anyone who lived or worked regularly with Appleby must need the patience of Job; he didn't think he could last a week without getting fidgety.

He drove to the Embankment and then over Battersea Bridge, less to test the police who were blocking the bridge at the other end than to drive in a roundabout way to the East End, covering the area where the Prowler had struck. There was one good thing: the Prowler wouldn't strike again tonight. His activities always finished soon after eleven o'clock. From now on the night should be one of straight routine, except the East End gang job, the tail end of the hunt for the Prowler, and anything he didn't know about.

The last affected Gideon as much as anything: the countless crimes being committed at that moment, cloaked by London's darkness. Four out of five of the night's offenses would not be discovered until next morning, and, as he drove, he was probably passing a dozen crimes actually being committed, yet was oblivious to them all.

Now, his mood was reflective and mellow.

A three minutes' hold-up at the far side of the bridge where two cars in the other direction were stopped by the police, their drivers being questioned and their shoes examined, cheered him further. No one would get through the cordon easily. Probably thousands of motorists had been stopped, hundreds of buses held up; the old job of looking for a needle in a haystack was on again. But they'd found at least one needle tonight.

So as he headed toward the East End his thoughts were easier than they had been for some time. Willy Smith had high hopes for his daughter. Willy and the lectures, too—good idea, those lectures, it wouldn't be amiss to have them at all the Divisions. Might be a good idea to make them a bit more interesting than the usual run, and pep things up a bit. Get a couple of crime reporters to talk on the newspaper angle of crimes, for instance, a pathologist or two for the grisly stuff; that always went down well, put a bit of humor into it. Willy was right in one way; the uniformed branch had a heavy rate of loss by resignation, and the Force's manpower position was going to be really acute before long. The plain-clothes branch was always kept at full strength and there were those—including people at the Home Office, who ought to know better—who thought that if the C.I.D. was at full strength everything in the garden was lovely, and the conquest of crime should be well on the way.

Idiots.

The conquest of crime wasn't the C.I.D.'s job. Conquest began before a crime was committed—conquest would have begun with Mrs. Golightly, for instance, if her husband hadn't left her on her own. The conquest of crime was simply a matter of prevention, and the job of the C.I.D. wasn't triumph over crime but a war against the criminals after they'd done their job. The real fight to win began with the uniformed men out on the beat—men like that chap Rider. And the uniformed branch was at least forty per cent under-staffed because they couldn't get enough of the right men to stay.

Was better pay the answer?

It might be part of it; that was all. The job wasn't really attractive yet, there weren't enough youngsters who felt like young Matthew. That gave him a warm glow. Here in the small hours, driving through the quiet with his headlights behaving as if they were driving the fog away in writhing defeat, he could feel the satisfaction at knowing that Matthew wanted to follow him at the Yard. It ought to be possible to persuade him to sit for the university scholarship, and make him realize that he would do much better for himself in the Yard's legal department, for instance; but if he did start out as a copper—

Gideon put the thought aside as he crossed Lambeth Bridge, was held up for a minute, then drove past the yard. The radio kept silent, so there wasn't much doing; Appleby would make sure that he was kept informed.

He thought again, in the mellowed, untroubled mood, of the crimes that were being committed now and would not come to light until later, and he felt almost philosophical, so deep had been his relief at the finding of the Harris child.

He was quite right about one thing: about the crimes being committed within a stone's throw of him as he had driven through the streets of London.

Among the men who had seen his car drive past, and who had crouched out of sight until there was no danger of him being seen, was the Prowler. He was still inside the cordon, still in greater danger than he knew.

Among the women whom Gideon had passed was Mrs. Michael (Netta) Penn, until recently of 11 Lassiter Street.

When she had telephoned the Yard, she had simply been worried and distressed; when Gideon's car passed within a hundred yards of the cellar where she was sitting, she was terrified.

For a long time she had gone on searching for her husband, always desperately, fearful of the reason for his disappearance. She had never found the courage to speak of it to the police, but she was frightened in case her husband, her beloved Michael, had been murdered. She had believed that, if she could persuade Scotland

Yard to look for him, they would find out the best or the worst.

That night, in the fog, she had telephoned Scotland Yard, asking for Gideon because Gideon's name had been in the newspapers several times recently and had grown tired of talking to casual telephone men with indifferent voices, to officials who obviously thought that she was making a lot of fuss about nothing.

Two or three things that Michael had said before his disappearance had suggested that he was going to some money; he had talked of "being rich." So she connected his disappearance with new-found wealth. She was absolutely certain he would not just walk out of her life; that if it was humanly possible he would telephone or write to her.

So—he *must* be dead.

He had been so happy, so confident in his love.

Among the people she had talked to about Michael had been the Rikkers of 11 Lassiter Street. She had called there tonight, before telephoning, to inquire for letters and messages—praying for one from Michael.

There had been none.

Rikker, the landlord, a middle-aged man she had never liked, had been harsh and unfriendly, and his drab of a wife no better. Without realizing that it was the first time she had told them this, she had said that she was going to make the police look for Michael; that very night she was going to telephone Gideon.

Before Gideon had come on the line, while she had been waiting with a new sort of hope, Rikker had loomed out of the fog, opened the kiosk door, and twisted the telephone out of her hand.

"You come with me," he had said, and the night had muffled his voice and her fears had stifled hers.

Now she was in terror, because she was sure that they had killed Michael and they were going to kill her.

128

11

Night of Terror

It was a small house. Sounds would travel from it easily. It was possible to hear the rumble of the buses from the main road which ran along one end, and the cars which passed, too. It was also an old house, and had a cellar deep beneath the ground, with only a round hatch leading to the pavement through which sound could escape. The hatch was covered, the boxes standing beneath it and sacking stuffed tightly between the top box and the hatch, so that no sound escaped.

Netta sat on an upright chair in the cellar, and she was tied to it with rope which she couldn't loosen, and which hurt her arms and cut into her thighs. One light burned above her head, but it was chance that it shone almost directly into her eyes, making them water, making her long to close them—although she dared not close them for long, in case she lost consciousness and so missed any sound or sight to indicate that the landlord was coming back.

She did not know how long she had been here.

There had been the telephone kiosk, the opening door, the landlord's powerful grasp, her fear, the way he had hustled her back to Number 11, with a scarf round her face so that, even if she had wanted to scream, she could not. The night had been thick with fog and empty of people, and she had been bundled over the threshold of the house where she had once had her home in two furnished rooms upstairs.

Then, she had been wildly happy.

Now—

Rikker had taken her downstairs into the cellar, his wife had followed and, when the door at the foot of the stairs had closed on them, she had realized how utterly silent it was down here. In part, that might be due to the stillness of the night, but here were the bricks of the walls, whitewashed, looking big and solid.

One big section looked new. The floor was solid concrete. In one corner, beneath the manhole, there was a heap of coke, for burning.

They had questioned her, first the man, and then his wife.

How often had she been to the police? What had she told the police? Why had she gone to the police?

How often?

What had she told them?

Why had she gone?

First the man and then the woman had thrown the same question at her, the man roughly, the woman in a whining, pleading tone; and in a way she liked the woman less and feared her more than Rikker, a thickset, powerful man, wearing a heavy sailor's sweater of navy blue, who needed a shave. All the time she had lived in the two rooms upstairs he had needed one; occasionally he rasped thick, horny fingers over the gray stubble, and on his breath lay the strong odor of whisky.

How often . . . What . . . Why?

At first her mind had been paralyzed by fear and she

told them the simple truth, time and time again. She had telephoned the police six or seven times; she couldn't be sure how many. She had told them that Michael had disappeared, and that she was sure that something had happened to him. And she had telephoned them because she was certain that Michael wouldn't just have walked out on her; he had been too much in love.

And he had.

She could picture him now, with thick, fair hair which curled a little and the smile in his eyes and his rather snubbed nose and his gentle hands.

How often?

What?

Why?

"I've told you!" she burst out at last. "I keep telling you; why do you want to know?"

They hadn't told her.

They had left her tied to the chair and gone out, letting the heavy wooden door swing to behind them, and with the unshaded electric lamp just above and just in front of her eyes, so that it hurt to look at it, and she could never escape from the glare.

At first she hadn't been able to forget the questions. It was as if her mind had received an image—as the eye received the image of the filament of the electric lamp—and, even when the questions had stopped, she had echoed them. Fear had been her dominant emotion then, and in a way it still was, but then she had not known the root causes of her fear; now she did.

They had killed Michael.

They would kill her.

There was no way of being absolutely sure, but she felt sure. They were frightened too; they had been frightened of what she might have told the police, and she had told them nothing—*nothing*. She had not dreamed that the Rikkers knew anything about Michael's disappearance. He had left for his office one day, and for weeks afterward she had lived on the memory of the way he had promised that before long he would get her out of these two furnished rooms into a real home of their own. It had been a blissful day, but—

He had not come home.

She had been out that afternoon, visiting her mother, who lived in Horley Street, Fulham, not far. She had not reached Lassiter Street until seven o'clock, and had quite expected Michael to be home, but—she had never seen him again.

She had telephoned his office, and been told that he had left at the usual time; that was all.

He hadn't gone back to the office, either.

When the Rikkers had told her that she must leave the two rooms, she had been alarmed because Michael wouldn't know at once where to get in touch with her. She had gone to stay with her mother, who knew what had happened. And she had got a job. Life had gone on, drably, emptily, and once a week she called at 11 Lassiter Street to see if there were any letters, or if Michael had come back. The Rikkers knew her new address, but she had sensed they had no liking for her, and she hadn't trusted them to forward letters or any messages. She had been right not to; several times she had found letters addressed to Michael. Nothing much but—

All of these things went through her mind while she was alone in the cold, bare, almost soundproof cellar.

The cold bit into her.

Now and again she began a shivering fit which she could not control. Her feet were so cold that they

132

ached, her fingers so cold that she felt as if they would snap if anyone bent them. The ropes round her arms and body, and over her thighs, made all movement difficult except that of her head. Once or twice, she had fancied that she heard a sound, but nothing had followed it.

Now she sat terrified. Yet she was falling into a kind of stupor—the bright light, the lamp filament, the shiny glass pear shape of the lamp, the thick walls, the cold, the aching, the images of questions—*how often, what, why?*

Now and again her head drooped with exhaustion, but each time she woke in panic and moved her head about wildly, to wake herself up, for there was the great fear in her—that if she went to sleep she might not wake again.

Upstairs, in a small back room, with a kitchen table and an electric stove, two old saddleback chairs and several wooden chairs, a big deal dresser and some prints taken from the tops of tradesmen's calendars, the Rikkers sat and drank—Rikker whisky, his wife gin. Looking at them and forgetting the white and black of the big stove, it was easy to imagine that a hundred years had passed this room by. This might be a thieves' kitchen drawn by Boz and peopled by Dickens. Rikker, barrel-like and massive with a flat head and a low forehead, his wife small and flat breasted, with greasy gray hair.

In a corner was a big, new television set. It had not been there when Netta and Michael Penn had lived in the two rooms above.

In a cupboard beneath the dresser were seven bottles of whisky; single half-bottles had been the rule before the Penns had "left."

133

The Rikkers had not said a great deal, and the television had been on most of the evening although they had not taken much notice of it; the noise was in the background, that was all.

Every now and again, Mrs. Rikker had said:

"What are you going to *do* with her?"

Rikker hadn't once answered.

Then, halfway through the evening, there had come a sharp knock at the front door, making Rikker jump to his feet, sending his wife cringing in alarm. The knock had been repeated. Rikker had told his wife to stay in the kitchen, with the door closed, and had gone out. His wife would probably have collapsed, but Rikker had answered the detective's questions gruffly but civilly enough. Yes, Penn had left months ago, Mrs. Penn weeks ago. Why? She couldn't pay her rent. Did he know why Penn had left her? Usual reasons, Rikker supposed; he got fed up. Had he seen Penn since he had left? No.

No, no, no, no.

After the man had gone, apparently satisfied, Rikker had returned to the kitchen and poured himself too much whisky and tossed it down.

"Who—who was it, Rikky?"

"Never you mind."

"Rikky, who was it?"

"Shut your trap!"

"Rikky, was it—was it the *police?*"

He'd swallowed more whisky. She had stood on the other side of the table, out of hand's reach if he should move to strike her, but with her eyes wide open and rounded, and her thin lips parted to show unnaturally even, white teeth; a young woman's teeth in an old woman's face.

"Rikky! Was it a copper?"

"I told you to shut your bloody trap."

134

"I want to know who it was. Was it a copper? What did he want, what—"

"I told you to shut your *trap.*" Rikker hissed, and he leaned forward and struck at her, but she dodged and he missed. "So a copper came and asked some questions. So what? He came to ask if she still lived here, and I told him she didn't, we hadn't seen her for weeks. That was nearly the truth, wasn't it? What difference does it make?"

The woman's face looked much, much older.

"Why—why do you think the copper came, Rikky?"

"She called the cops, didn't she?"

"Do you—do you think she said anything—"

"I told you before, she didn't *know* anything, so how could she tell the cops anything? She was just worried because Penn didn't come back, that's all. If she'd kept her nose out of my business—" Rikker broke off, as if even he realized that the remark was the ultimate absurdity.

There had been a long silence. Then:

"What—what are you going to do with her?" Mrs. Rikker asked hoarsely.

"The same as we did with him, what do you think we're boing to do?" Rikker rasped. "But I'm not taking no chances. I'm going to make sure the cops don't come back before I get the job done."

There had been another long silence, and then:

"She—she ain't done us any harm, Rikky, do you think—"

"If she gets the police looking for Penn she'll get us caught on a murder rap, that's how much harm she can do. Now shut your gob, you always talk to much."

Silence.

"Rikky."

Silence.

"Rikky, do you think the police will come again?"

135

"What I think is I've had enough from you tonight, I'm going out for a walk," Rikker said roughly. He stood up, finished the whisky in his glass, and then went out, taking a thick topcoat off a peg behind the door. His wife first watched and then went after him, but he didn't look round.

Then, the fog had been at its thickest.

Rikker had met a neighbor, coming home from the pub, and the neighbor had told him that the police were after someone in a big way; a man in the pub had been held up at a station, someone else in a bus on Westminster Bridge. Something about a baby. And something about a girl.

"Rikky," his wife had muttered when he had got back, "when are you going to do it?"

"I'll take my time."

"How—are you—"

"I'm going to do what I did the last time," Rikker said. "I'm going to knock her over the head, see, so she won't feel anything. Then I'm going to brick her up in the wall, the same as I did him. Any more questions?"

"You—you won't *hurt* her, will you?"

Then he had struck her across the face before she could dodge, grabbed her shoulders and shaken her until her teeth rattled and her head bobbled up and down. When his rage had subsided, he had pushed her away and she had slumped back on the sofa, half crying. He had poured himself another drink, then gone to the cellar door.

Gideon passed within a hundred yards of the house, and drove with his new-found sense of quiet satisfaction toward the East End and the gangs. This led

136

him through the deserted city, its dark buildings tall against the sky, the Bank of England squat and forbidding on its corner, the Stock Exchange looking as if the Greeks had built it there.

Along Throgmorton Street, two cars were parked, with their side lights on, and in the building by them a light shone out at the third floor.

"Fog's practically gone," Gideon said to himself, and drove on, thinking that someone else was working late.

In the room from which the light shone out above Throgmorton Street, two men were sitting. Both were young-middle-aged. One was portly and pale, the other slim and hardy looking, carrying the tan of long hours in the sun; this made his gray eyes seem very bright and gave him a handsomeness which made the other man look nondescript. Both were well dressed and prosperous looking. They sat in an office with paneled walls, near a large polished desk with a swivel chair behind it. For some time they had been sitting in large armchairs, whisky decanter and soda siphon on a small table between them, and papers spread out on the floor all around them.

It was very quiet.

A car passed in the street, making a purring note; the bright-eyed man didn't notice it, but the other looked up sharply.

The bright-eyed man said, "Not nervous, George, are you?"

"Nervous? Me? Don't be silly, Paul. I never was the nervous type." George Warren gave a quick grin and picked up his glass a little too quickly. "If I've got anything to be nervous about, it's you."

"I don't get you," Paul Devereaux said easily.

Warren's smile became too quick and bright.

137

"Forget it, I only meant that I'll be down the drain if I don't get a hundred thousand out of this, and you're the strength of the deal. That's all I've got to be nervous about. I've done my part." He picked up some thick documents and rustled them as if they were massive five-pound notes. "Share certificates in uranium ore found in the Lombo district of East Africa, where we have exclusive mineral rights *and* cheap labor. The uranium's there, too; any test will show it." He gave a quick little teetering laugh. "After all, you put it there! No doubt you planted it well, is there, Paul?"

"I planted it so that no one could dream that it didn't belong," Devereaux said. His bright eyes flashed, but he still looked a little wary. "In a day or two we'll get the prospector's report with everything confirmed, then we'll go to town with the new company."

"That's what I mean by my share," said Warren. "I've been doing a little discreet whispering already—hinting that something big is coming out of Warren and Company in the near future. Whisper it, though; don't let a good thing pass on to the other chaps, you know. I've had a dozen discreet inquiries to deal with already. If I'd cared to I could have collected the hundred thousand before issuing the shares. That's how high the integrity of Warren and Company stands!" He rubbed his hands together. "If that prospecting report is fully substantiated, we'll offer the shares for private sale, without any publicity. And everyone concerned will think he's on a bargain! I'll warn them that it will be five years before they see any big returns, too."

"Sounds like a cakewalk," said Devereaux, and poured himself another drink. "There's one little thing you won't forget, isn't there?"

"What's that?"

"You owe me ten thousand pounds and expenses."

"My dear chap, you'll have it within forty-eight hours of the new issue being offered!" said Warren. "That's a first charge." He seemed to have overcome his nervousness, and had a little color in his plump cheeks. "What are you going to do after this?"

Devereaux grinned.

"I'm going to be a playboy for six months, and make as many girls as I can provided they don't want me to run to mink. After that—well, I'll probably go exploring again!" He stood up and went to the window, saying. "It's time we went, George. Belinda will be wondering where you are."

"She can wonder," George Warren said abruptly. "If it wasn't for Belinda I wouldn't have got so heavily into debt, but—" He shrugged a gloomy thought off. "I've brought five years- reprieve, anyhow, and anything can happen in that time. Why, there might even be uranium in the Lombo district!"

"George, what was worrying you just now?" asked Devereaux quietly.

After a pause, Warren said abruptly, "I was wondering what Belinda would do if this was ever found out. She'd rob anybody if she could, but if there was any risk of being put in jail—"

"The worst that can happen is that the uranium doesn't pan out so well. It won't be the first hush-hush proposition that fell flat," said Devereaux. "You'll only collect from the get-rich-quick boys, anyhow."

Warren nodded and they began to tidy up the office.

12

East End

Gideon received a radio message as he neared Aldgate, telling him that Hemmingway and Lemaitre were in a street near the gymnasium where one of the gangs had gathered. He knew the place slightly—as he knew nearly everything which had the remotest association with London's crime. The gymnasium had once been a genuine part of dockland, giving stevedores, sailors and the local inhabitants a place to show their paces, have a turn with the gloves, the rope or the wall bars. The then owners had made a grave mistake by arranging to get a license, and, soon after beer and spirits became available in the bar, the quality of the patrons began to fall, although some old habitues had continued to come in order to drink at prices slightly below that of nearby public houses.

Then the Wide boys had moved in.

The gymnasium had several advantages for a gang. It was on the ground floor of an old warehouse, plenty large enough for a crowd to meet, and the Wide boys had nearly fifty associate members. It offered, through the ring and the fixtures, a meeting place which was ostensibly a physical-training club, so that no one could object to it, not even the police. Although officially it was illegal to sell beer after eleven o'clock at night, there was nothing against keeping the club open all night, if the members wanted it. A piano had been brought in, there were half a dozen amateur musicians including a surprisingly good drummer in the club and, as the warehouse was not in a residential district, music and dancing often went on for most of the night.

Not a hundred yards from the gymnasium was the old Dockside Club. This had a similar history, except that it had been a youth club for the thousands of young people who grew up in the sprawling mass of tiny, crowded airless streets which led off the docks. It had existed for years, sometimes flourishing, more often than not just surviving, until the Melky gang had taken it over.

They had done so quite legally, for the Melky gang was remarkable because most of its members were very young. Even Melky, the absolute boss, was only twenty-two—although he had been married five years and had three children by a sexy little Italian girl who was said to be the brains behind him. The members of the gang had joined the club at a time when it had been run jointly by a Church of England and a nonconformist church; within six months the church influence had vanished completely, but all the club facilities remained. There were indoor games, a movie projector and screen, a television room, even an arts and crafts room, but there was no license for liquor.

Although the law was broken frequently in both establishments, and although occasionally members of the rival gangs would clash and there would be a bloodied nose or two, the general behavior of the gangs in London was reasonably good. Certainly there was no plausible excuse for the police to close down either of the places. Melky's gang worked the race-courses within easy reach south of London, and the Wide boys went northwest. They both worked the crowds—picking pockets, stealing winnings, snatching handbags—and the usual protection method was adopted; one or two of the "boys" worked while half a dozen stood by to make sure that if there was trouble the others could get away. Occasionally a member of the gang was picked up for being in possession of stolen goods, but, if one was sent inside, his wife or family was looked after by the gang.

Each gang had boasted of its size and strength.

Each had grown stronger in the past twelve months.

Recently, Melky's gang had appeared on the same race courses as the Wide boys. That seemed the end of the unwritten agreement, and that was why Hemmingway was so worried about what might happen. He knew—and Gideon knew—that if there was a running fight through the docks, enormous damage could be done to warehouses, stored goods and even to ships themselves. When gangs really got out of control, it was dangerous and could be deadly.

Gideon caught sight of a policeman in a doorway as he slowed down in the street where he was to meet Hemmingway and Lemaitre. He stopped just in front of the corner and got out, aware of being watched, but seeing no one. There was no other car in sight. Just across the intersecting road there was the tall wall of a warehouse, and a hundred yards or so away there were the lighted windows of the old Dockside Club, in another nearby warehouse.

A man approached.

"That you, George?" It was Lemaitre, who sounded quite brisk.

"Yes."

"Hemmingway's gone round the back way to have a

look at things near the Red Lion Gymnasium," Lemaitre said. "He'll be back in a few minutes. We've got all the streets sealed off, but there are between a hundred and a hundred and forty louts in those two clubs, and they're all spoiling for a fight. You can tell it a mile off. We've got about forty men, and they're spread thin."

And a hundred or more were waiting at bridges and other vantage points in the nearly forlorn hope of catching the Prowler.

"We'll get some more," promised Gideon. "Got the entrances to the docks covered?"

"As far as we can," said Lemaitre. "Don't want to push you, George, but if you could send for those reinforcements you'd do me and Hemmingway a lot of good."

"Let's fix it," Gideon said flatly.

They went to his car, and he leaned inside and flicked on the radio telephone, ignoring the noises as they came crackling in. As he waited for the Information Room to answer, he recalled the way he had been stopped at the bridge, told himself that it was idiocy to believe that the Prowler might still be trapped inside the cordon. It was after two o'clock! He ought to have had the reinforcements here an hour or more ago; certainly he ought to have trusted Hemmingway's judgment.

Even so, he was reluctant to give the order.

He gave it.

As he moved from the car, another approached along the street he had come along; it stopped behind him and Hemmingway got out, bustling.

"You, George?"

"Yes."

"If you don't—"

"I have," said Gideon.

144

"'Bout time, too," said the NE Divisional Superintendent, although obviously he was mollified on the instant. "I've just been round to the east-side gates—or where they would be if there were any! They've taken the actual gates down to let in some of the big stuff that's due in by road, so all we've got up is a flimsy wooden barrier. The two night-duty gatemen have got the breeze up properly; they say they can smell this fight the way you can smell the eucalyptus a hundred miles away from the coast of Australia."

Gideon said blankly, "Can you?"

Hemmingway chuckled, yet gave the impression that he was very much on edge.

"I read it in a book," he announced. "How much did Lemaitre tell you? There are all of a hundred and twenty rats waiting to mix it."

"Any idea why they've waited so long?"

"One side's waiting for the other to move," Hemmingway said, "that's all."

Earlier in the evening, Gideon had wondered whether this situation was as simple as it had seemed, but first Hemmingway and then Lemaitre had persuaded him that it was. Now his doubts came back. There had been fights before. He couldn't recall that any of them had started in the small hours, although often the fights lasted until dawn, the protagonists splitting up into groups which grew smaller and smaller. Tonight's behavior was peculiar. Everyone on the spot seemed quite certain what was on foot, but—

"Heard one rumor that could explain it," said Hemmingway.

"What's that?"

"After Melky's boys wouldn't stop poaching, the Wide boys tried to kidnap his pocket Lollo. They failed, but they said that if Melky didn't call his men out of their grounds, they'd get her."

145

"Where is Lollo?"

"In the old Dockside Club."

"Sure?"

"She was seen to arrive, just before twelve o'clock, with an escort of six of the biggest members of the gang."

"Hmm," said Gideon, and scratched the back of his neck.

It was quite obvious that Hemmingway planned to seal off all the entrances and exits to the area, and then let the two gangs fight it out. If it worked that way, then probably each gang would be so weakened that the police could step in and finish things off, arrest the gang leaders on charges which should put them in jail for twelve months at least, and so put an end to their activities for a long time. It was the kind of clear-up that the police liked and which they were able to fix now and again on a comparatively small scale; but Gideon didn't feel at ease over this.

"What's on your mind?" Lemaitre knew him well enough to sense his doubts.

Gideon grunted noncommittally.

In the distance he heard several cars, and realized that these were the first of the patrol cars which had come off the Prowler job; they hadn't taken long. Well, that was over and done with, for tonight, and this now seemed the only urgent issue.

"Give," urged Lemaitre.

"Dunno," said Gideon, and looked at Hemmingway's strong, big features. "Ever know them to wait for as long as this to start something? Don't hear anything, do you?"

"Bit of singing earlier, but it quieted down," conceded Hemmingway. "But—"

"All right, I'm stubborn," Gideon said almost roughly, "but if there's going to be a schemozzle

146

between the gangs we usually hear them getting warmed up first—they get tiddly, then they get tight, they start singing and banging the piano about. Then they send out one or two scouts, to call the other side a lot of so-and-sos, and soon they can't hold themselves in any longer and start with the razors and the knuckle dusters."

Hemmingway almost jeered. "You must have been reading a book, too."

"Anything wrong?"

"Elementary, my dear Gee-Gee."

"Why aren't they drunk tonight?" asked Gideon.

"Serious business afoot."

"As you said earlier, when they really get mad with each other they lose every bit of sense they ever had," said Gideon. "Hemmy, know what I'd like to do?"

"Listen, George, we can't start the raid; so far they haven't done a thing to give us an excuse. If we start it, they'll be fresh and they'll probably join forces against us, and our chaps—"

"I'd like you to go and talk to the Wide boys' chief, while I go and talk to Melky."

There was a startled pause. More cars sounded in the distance, for London at night was very quiet and no ships near this section of the docks were being worked. Some way off, floodlights shining on the spindly cranes on deck and the heavier ones alongside showed clearly.

Even the river was now clear of fog, and there was a freshening breeze.

Two cars turned the corner and came along slowly.

"You crazy?" Hemmingway demanded at last.

"Nothing crazy about it," said Gideon. "We just tell them that we don't like what they're up to, and they're to go home."

"Goddammit, George, they're inside their own premises. You can't even pretend you think they're going to cause a breach of the peace; you wouldn't have a legal leg to stand on." Hemmingway stared up at Gideon, who stood still and quiet and yet somehow dominant, by far the largest man in the little group which had been enlarged by the men now arriving from the Squad cars which had been at the bridges. "You really mean it, don't you?" Hemmingway added in a resigned tone. "But I'm telling you that it won't make any difference."

"You may be right," Gideon said. "Let's go."

"Alone?"

"If they're fighting mad the sight of half a dozen coppers will just about set 'em alight, but we'd better go in pairs. Lemaitre can come with me, and you take a chap. Send for him and then let's go ahead," added Gideon. He walked on, while Hemmingway gave an order, then hurried to catch up. Lemaitre and Hemmingway's aide, a detective inspector, walked behind them through the gloom.

Hemmingway was breathing hard, as if fighting back antagonism.

"Got an idea I didn't want to talk about in front of the others," Gideon said to him. "If it's any good, it'll be better if it comes from you."

"It won't, if it's anything like the rest of your ideas tonight!"

Gideon chuckled.

Ahead, a little man who was watching from the corner moved out of sight, obviously to go and report to his boss that the two men were approaching. Gideon felt quite sure that the members of both gangs were fully aware that the police were concentrating, and that the little shadowy figure was one of several scouts. He didn't go on at first, but their footsteps were heavy and clear in the street, and seemed to echo off the high warehouse wall.

"All right, let's have it," said Hemmingway.

"What ships are tied up at these docks?" asked Gideon.

"*Norda,* registered at Oslo, *Marianne* from Antwerp, *Black Marquis* from New Orleans, and a thing with a name I can't pronounce, from Cairo. But what—"

"They discharging or loading cargo?"

"The *Norda*'s loading, ready to sail in the morning," said Hemmingway. "I don't know about the *Marianne. Black Marquis* has just arrived; so has the Egyptian ship." Hemmingway scratched the back of his head, and they slowed down as they neared the corner. A shadow was thrown across the road telling them that a man was just round the corner, probably judging their progress from the sound of their approach. "Don't ask me what they're carrying; I'm not a walking encyclopedia." He sounded aggressive, and that was probably because Gideon had made him uneasy. "What's on your mind?"

"Both gangs out in strength, dock gates off and unprotected, suspicious quiet and a motive for a row which doesn't stand up," said Gideon.

"You're wrong there. Melky's so jealous that—"

"If anyone made a pass at his wife he'd try to cut them up without having a cold-blooded, full-scale gang war," said Gideon, "and I think that this is a put-up job for us to swallow. I'd like to know what's in the holds of those ships, or what's going in."

"I can soon find out," Hemmingway said, very slowly and uneasily. "I can call the dock police; they'll know. Let's get this job over quick. Sure you prefer to take Melky?"

"Positive."

"You know he's got a reputation for—"

"He won't use a knife on me or anyone else tonight,"

149

said Gideon. "I'll take Lemaitre, you take your chap."

They reached the corner. The scout just round the corner vanished inside the entrance of the gymnasium, and along the street were the lights of the other club. Not fifty yards beyond it, where a single lamp burned in the archway, were the "gates" leading to the docks; the opening was very wide, and the only sign of life was in a small gate office, where a light burned yellow.

Just beyond this office a dozen policemen were out of sight.

Lemaitre caught Gideon up.

"Any special angle, George?"

"Just see how it goes," said Gideon.

So he went in.

At that very moment, some miles away, the Prowler hid in a doorway, near a tube station which was still open. He saw a police car, which had been standing there over two hours, move off at speed.

At the same time, nearer to Gideon, Paul Devereaux and George Warren got into their respective cars and also drove off.

At Scotland Yard, the Information Room buzzed with messages both in and out, the blocks of wood which represented patrol cars were being moved all the time, the greatest concentration being now about the East End and the NE Division. But news of burglaries, two with violence, of fires, of smash-and-grab raids, of streetwalking, of car thefts, of almost every crime in the calendar came streaming in. Appleby and a sergeant were in Gideon's office, sending out instructions, sorting out everything that had to be done, assigning men to the various jobs on which the Divisions needed specialist help.

Approaching Scotland Yard in a police car was M. Monnet, of the *Sureté Nationale,* with a small black brief case under his arm, a small cigar between his lips, a Homburg hat at the back of his head, a smooth-cloth coat buttoned tightly about him.

At London airport the indignant—and possibly frightened—Leslie Forrester argued with the Customs, who were making a thorough search of everything he had brought with him, and yet were so pleasant and apologetic.

And in the cellar at 11 Lassiter Street, little Netta Penn sat as if her body were turned to ice, with pain at her eyes and numb dread in her heart. She couldn't even wriggle her fingers now, she was so cold.

For the past hour, she had heard sounds of scratching and faint banging, and at one time she thought these were a long way off. In fact they were close to her—and she knew that Rikker was doing something to the wall of the cellar, on the other side of the door.

She didn't know what.

In the space of fifteen minutes, seven Flying Squad and three patrol cars passed the end of Lassiter Street.

13

Melky

As Gideon stepped inside the doorway of the old Dockside Club, beneath a dirty, tattered banner which hadn't been taken down and reading YOUTH FOR CHRIST CRUSADE, he heard music—hot jazz probably coming from a radiogram or a record player. Two members of the Melky gang were in the doorway which led to the main room of the club, where the lights were bright and the music was loud, and shuffle of feet suggested that a few couples were dancing. Someone began to sing the lyrics in a shrill flat voice. The two youths, dark haired, pale faced and wary, were dwarfed by Gideon as he approached them. They seemed ready to try to bar his way, but he walked as if he hadn't noticed them; either he would bump into them or they would move aside.

They moved.

Gideon went into the big room first, and Lemaitre followed, also ignoring the two doormen.

A few tawdry decorations including colored toy balloons, many of them deflated, hung from the ceiling. At the end of the hall on a high stage was a girl in a strapless "gown," which covered just about as much of her as a two-piece bathing suit, swaying in front of a microphone which obviously didn't work. By her side were a record player and a youth with a shock of ginger hair swaying to the rhythm. The smell of tobacco smoke was thick and acrid. Three couples danced, hugging each other. Sitting at small tables round the walls were most of the members of the gang—nearly all young and sallow, some obviously not English, others as native Cockney as Bow Bells. Most of them were dressed in old clothes, and not to kill, which by itself was an indication that they hadn't come simply for a good time. Most appeared to be drinking soft drinks, but in some of the glasses there was undoubtedly hard liquor. At one corner there was a snack bar, where a blousy girl wriggled and giggled with two boys who had come to "help" serve, and were pretty rough. Underneath smeary glass covers were sandwiches and sausage rolls, and attached to the wall was a steaming tea or coffee urn.

About the middle of one wall, at the biggest table in the hall, sat Melky—or Antonio Melcrino—and with him was his Lollo. Her name was not Lollo—when Gideon had first heard of her it had been Maria—but she had a figure which matched the fabulous Lollo's, and so had taken the name. She wore a tight-fitting, shiny black dress, obviously drawn tightly at the back to pull her stomach as flat as it could be, and to make her bust just out so much that she looked more caricature than a real person. She had a mass of dark curls, fine, dark, glowing eyes, and full, red lips; she was really something, and it was hard to realize that she was the mother of three children.

Melky sat beside her.

He was third-generation London Italian. His mother and father kept a small cafe in Kensington, and had only one sorrow: the fact that their son had gone bad. He hadn't visited them for years. He was short and thin, with a sharp-featured, sensitive-looking face. His hair was not particularly dark, and was silky and brushed straight back from a high forehead. If one saw him in the street and guessed what he did for a living, it would be easy to suggest that he was an intellectual or an artist. The only artistry he knew was with the knife. He could carve patterns on human skin and, when the mood took him, pieces out of human flesh.

Now he sat, not really truculent, not sullen, simply wary—like everyone else here. His knife wasn't in sight.

The music stopped.

Melky did not motion to the red-haired boy on the stage, but another record went on, and the singer swayed and rolled her eyes and began to sing again. This was prearranged, of course; they weren't going to let the police think they could interfere or scare them.

Gideon stopped in front of the big table.

He glanced at Lollo, then took his hat off, a completely unexpected gesture, and he nodded to her as he might to any woman whom he met casually.

"Tony Melcrino?" he asked.

"That's me," Melky said, hardly moving his thin lips.

"What's going on tonight?"

"We're celebrating," Melky said.

"Bit late, aren't you?"

"My mother said I could stay up late," said Melky, and there was a slight relaxation in the attitude of the people about him; one boy laughed. The dancing couples contrived to mark time near the table, and over by the bar the giggling girl was standing still, each boy with an arm round her, all three staring toward Gideon.

"You can make it funny or you can take it straight," Gideon said. "I don't care how you take it, but if you

155

know what's good for you you'll break this party up."

"What am I doing?" demanded Melcrino, and glanced up at Lollo and thrust out his chest. "Minding my own, that's all. Pity other people don't follow my example."

Gideon just stared at him.

The man wasn't really at ease, but he wasn't worried either; he was completely assured of his position here, and he had sound legal cause to be. Hemmingway was probably having the same kind of interview with the leader of the Wide boys and telling himself that it was all a waste of time.

"Close the door when you go out," Melcrino said, and this time half a dozen of his followers made giggly noises.

"Listen to me, Melcrino," Gideon said, and stood so that he could see not only the man himself but also his wife who had pulled a chair a little closer. "If you start a fight tonight you'll bite off more than you can chew. I'm warning you. Tell your boys to go home." He paused, and he saw the glint in Melcrino's eyes, and saw the way Lollo squeezed his hand; they thought they were so clever and yet were such naive fools. "Hemmingway's giving the Wide boys the same orders," Gideon went on. "If you two want to fight it out, choose somewhere else. This is my beat."

"And it's my business," Melky said sneeringly.

Gideon was quite sure that the glint in his eyes and the squeeze from his wife meant one thing: satisfaction, almost elation, and elation could only be due to something he had said. All he had said was that the police assumed that a gang fight was in the offing.

"Don't make us get rough," Gideon said.

"You couldn't hurt pussy," Melcrino sneered. "Think we're scared of a bunch of ruddy rozzers? Go and fry your face, Gideon, that's how frightened I am of *you*."

He moved his hand in a gesture which brought the loudest laugh so far. That was the moment when the music stopped, a moment when the situation could become ugly, but Gideon did not think it would be ugly just yet.

"All right," he said, as if frustrated, "I've warned you. I came myself because I wanted you to know that we're right behind Hemmingway. If you try to carve up the Wide boys, most of you will end up in the hospital or in the dock, and we'll make every charge stick."

"Peanuts," said Melcrino, and so elicited a roar of laughter.

There was a moment's pause; soon Gideon would retire with the jeers of the gang in his ears, and they would think that they had scored a signal triumph, that they could poke their noses at the police. It would really elate them and, when they came to act, it might easily make them careless.

Then Lollo Melcrino pushed her chair back, gave a broad, seductive smile, and stepped toward Gideon with her hands on her hips and her body swaying. She was the perfect subject for one of the illustrated tabloids, and in fact she was really quite beautiful; her shoulders and that part of her not covered by the dress were creamy and smooth and free from blemish. Her dark eyes glowed, and she just stood in front of Gideon, put her head on one side, and asked in a husky voice:

"Why don't you hit one of your own size?"

She stood lower than his massive chin.

The laughter seemed to shake the walls.

"Didn't get any change out of that," said Lemaitre. "If we don't slap them down after this our name will be mud." There was unspoken reproof in his voice.

"Thick mud," agreed Gideon. He didn't hurry back to the corner, for Hemmingway would probably be another ten minutes; he'd had further to go. The sound of music faded slightly. Above their heads the stars shone, and not far along the river there came the sharp blasts of a ship's siren; one of the smaller ships was about to leave the Port of London.

Gideon switched on the radio as he reached the car, and Lemaitre lit a cigarette and flicked the match moodily over the car's roof.

"Give me Mr. Appleby."

"Yes, sir."

"Hello, Cappen," greeted Appleby, obviously at his brightest. "Not forgotten the old folks at home? How are things out there?"

"Ominous."

"Well, we can't send anyone else," said Appleby. "We've had to rush the cars over to Hampstead; three burglaries on the Heath. Could be by the same man but it don't look like it. Bit of trouble in Mayling Square, too. Looks like a peeress has run off with a chauffeur, taking some of the heirlooms with them, and his nibs tried to shoot the lights out of them."

"Who is it?"

"Lord Addisal."

"Don't take any chances with that," said Gideon urgently. "Who've we got on duty? . . . Send Morley, He—"

"He's there. But we can't keep it quiet; the *Daily Wire*'s there too."

"Morley can handle it if anyone can," said Gideon. "We don't want a rap over the knuckles from the House of Lords, and—"

"Ever hear that fool story about one law for the poor and one for the rich?" asked Appleby brightly. "Ever hear such libelous nonsense? I've got M. Monnet

158

here—well, not exactly here, but downstairs waiting. What time will you be back?"

"Say half an hour, but don't keep him waiting too long."

"No, sir. That's about the lot," Appleby went on. "We're getting all the routine reports from the Divisions now. I'm telling the sarge to go through them and pick out anything he thinks worth looking at."

"Good," said Gideon.

Appleby was making sure that there could not be any cause for reproach, and he was proving almost exemplary in handling his job. Well, why not? A man could behave like a clown and still be a first-class detective. Take away Appleby's schoolboy sense of humor, and you had a man who ought to have been in or at least near his, Gideon's, shoes.

Gideon rang off.

"How's it going?" asked Lemaitre.

"Quietish. Trouble out at Hampstead," Gideon said, and saw Hemmingway and his sergeant turn the corner, walking very briskly. They had been longer even than he had expected, although he hadn't thought Hemmingway would spend a lot of time with the Wide boys. The two men came up. Hemmingway quickened his pace as he approached Gideon; the other man dropped behind.

"How'd it go?" asked Gideon.

"They just gave me a bit of lip," said Hemmingway gruffly. "If you ask me, when I told them to pack up and go home because we wouldn't stand for any gang fight, he was laughing up his sleeve. And do you know what I found out, George?"

"What?"

"The *Marianne*'s only waiting for her last load of cargo; it's due here any time. Not very big," declared Hemmingway, "just a few bags of mail. But some of the bags will contain registered packages, mostly British currency for banks in Belgium and Holland, a few containing commercial diamonds on their way to Holland." The NE man sounded bitter. "Not surprising I didn't tumble to it. The truth is that I didn't know the Post Office had started sending notes this way. They were sent by air until two weeks ago, when there were those thefts at the Hook."

"How do you think the gangs will play it?" asked Gideon.

"Why don't you finish the job?"

"Don't be a blurry fool. How do you think they'll play it?" demanded Gideon.

Hemmingway repeated, *"Blurry* fool; didn't you ever leave Sunday school?" and then his natural good humor asserted itself, and he went on more easily. "I think they'll be tipped off as soon as the van's on its way. They'll probably get a phone call. They'll start the riot then, but it'll be phony. They'll stop the van close to the *Marianne,* I should say, while we're sitting and waiting for them to cut themselves to pieces. At a signal they'll all pack it in and shake hands."

"Could be," agreed Gideon. "Well, it won't take much time to find out what route the Post Office van will take, and to make sure they don't get away with it. I'll have to leave it to you, though; I'm wanted back at the Yard. Going to stop and see the fun, Lem?"

"If you don't need me."

"Come and tell me how it goes when it's over," said Gideon. "Sorry I can't stop; there's a Frenchie here from Paris, wants us to extradite a chap who's just come over." He bent almost double so as to get into the car. "Mind Melky's wife," he said. "She'll cause more trouble than the rest of the gangs put together."

He heard their chuckles as he started the engine and drove off.

"If they come any better than Gee-Gee, I'd like to be there to see," said Hemmingway.

"If they come any better than Gee-Gee, I'd throw my hand in," Lemaitre said. "Better get cracking, hadn't we?"

A little over fifteen minutes later two more Squad cars passed the end of Lassiter Street, which was silent, like the rest of London.

Curiously, a little fog hung about here, although now there were very few traces. Not far away, Gideon drove for ten minutes through the empty streets, where every light seemed very bright, until he reached the Embankment. Soon he could see Big Ben, and gave himself a little personal eye test; he was able to pick out the time when he passed Charing Cross underground station, and rated that as good. He was even more comfortable in his mind than he had been when he had started out, and was resigned to the loss of the Prowler. There would be the East End mock fight to hand out to the press, the Harris baby rescue and two or three other successful jobs. There might be a few back-handers about the Prowler, but that was all. He turned into the gateway of the Yard at precisely ten minutes to three. Three Squad cars stood waiting, with their crews ready; when the reserve cars were down to three it really meant a busy night. He had a word with two of the detective inspectors in charge, then hurried up the stairs, up the lift, and along to his office. As he neared the door, he heard his name called from the corner.

"George."

He turned round, to see the lanky Gibb, from the laboratory, hurrying after him on his spindly legs. Gibb had taken off his white smock, and wore a baggy tweed jacket and a white collar which was several sizes too large for him. He had a theory that constriction of the throat by a tight collar and tie was a primary cause of early development of heart diseases.

"What've you got?" asked Gideon.

"That fingernail scraping, blood, Group O," said Gibb promptly, "and all the dope on the hair. How's the girl?"

"Don't know yet," said Gideon.

"Let me know," asked Gibb. "I'm just going downstairs for some eggs and bacon."

Gideon said, "Tell them I'll come down later if I can," and went to his own door and opened it.

His own French was fair, although he could understand others better than he could speak the language, but he wouldn't win a schoolboy's prize with his accent. As he opened the door two men were talking in French so fluent and flawless that it was hard to believe that they were not both Frenchmen.

One was M. Monnet, the other Appleby.

They were sitting on either side of Appleby's desk, talking nineteen to the dozen, the Frenchman's pale hands waving about all over the place, Appleby with one hand in his pocket. On telephone duty at Gideon's desk was the sergeant who had been in and out all evening—and in an odd way he surprised Gideon; he simply didn't register except as a piece of office furniture.

Neither of the men at the small desk heard the door open, but the sergeant jumped up.

Appleby was saying something; the Frenchman answered swiftly, then slapped his hands together and roared with laughter. Almost to Gideon's chagrin, the two men began to talk, one against the other, so fast that Gideon just couldn't pick out the meaning of what they said, only picked up a few words here and there.

Then he realized that they were exchanging unfamiliar phrases—Monnet in Paris argot, Appleby translating Cockney rhyming slang fairly liberally, and trotting it out as if French was his native language. Monnet was capping every phrase.

Gideon found himself chuckling.

Appleby looked up, startled, and then scrambled to his feet.

"Hello, hello, didn't see you! This is M. Monnet—"

The Frenchman got up nearly as quickly and bowed, a tall, immaculate young man with a smoothly clean-shaven face and, now, no hint of the laughter he had shown when talking to Appleby. He held out this hand.

"I am very happy to meet you." There was a slight precision of phrasing; otherwise his English was as good as his French. "You are Commander Gideon?"

"Yes." Gideon gripped a small, firm hand and waved to the sergeant. "Bring me up a chair." He saw the wariness spring to the Frenchman's eyes, and suspected that the man was uneasily aware that he might have annoyed Appleby's superior. "Glad to see you, M. Monnet, and before we go any further I've got one request to make."

The chair arrived.

"Yes, certainly, Mr. Gideon," said Monnet, while Appleby watched also with a kind of apprehension. One truth about Appleby was that even so near the retiring age he had an inferiority complex.

"We're going to speak English," said Gideon. "Exactly one minute ago I stopped thinking I could speak French."

Monnet relaxed, and threw up his hands, delighted.

"But it is not true, I have heard of your excellent French, Commander! But you are very kind. I am anxious, because—"

"Give me a minute," said Gideon, and looked at

163

Gideon. "Anything in from Brixton Hospital?"

"No change."

And no Prowler.

"Otherwise normal?"

"I should think so." Appleby slapped a hand on a sheaf of reports. "I haven't finished looking through the Divisional reports but if there was anything to worry about, they'd tell us."

"Good," said Gideon. "Now. M. Monnet . . ."

Among the reports on the desk was one from AB Division—Fulham. It said simply that a Mrs. Russell, of 21 Horley Street, had telephoned at two o'clock because she was worried about her daughter, a Mrs. Penn, who still hadn't returned home, although she would normally have arrived soon after ten o'clock. The report added that there had been no word at hospitals or police stations about a Mrs. Penn being involved in any accident.

14

M. Monnet

Spread out on Appleby's desk were the documents
which Monnet had brought with him. Most were in
French, but all had translation notes attached, and
Gideon read the notes rather than the originals. It was
apparent that the *Sureté Nationale* had long suspected
Leslie Forrester of the murder of the English girl in the
Hautes-Pyrenees, but there had been no firm evidence.
At the request of the authorities at Pau, Monnet had
been in charge of investigations. He had finally
collected a number of statements and much evidence,
including a photograph, that Forrester had been with
the girl in Pau three days before her body had been
found. Following that, there were some carefully
prepared statements and documents showing a pains-
taking collection of the evidence. Through all this there
were the indications that the *Sureté Nationale* had
made up its mind not to suggest that an Englishman
was involved until they were absolutely sure. That
evening, Monnet was to have charged Forrester.

The sergeant still acted as telephone boy, taking
messages and not once interrupting Gideon.

Gideon looked up from the documents.

"Does Forrester know you're after him?"

"That I cannot say," said Monnet. "It is peculiar, pairhaps that he should leave Paris tonight, but also, pairhaps not. He visits Paris on business four or five times a year, you see that, although only once had he been there this year, since the murder. His business, you will also see, is that of a commercial travelair; he represents a woolen manufacturair."

"Ever questioned him?"

"No, sir. But I have talked to the patron of the small hotel where he always stays, near St.-Germain-des-Près, and it is possible that the landlord has told him of the questions. That I do not know. What do you considair, Mr. Gideon? Is it sufficient evidence for Scotland Yard?"

"On the strength of this I'd recommend extradition," said Gideon, "but we'd have to hear what the chap's got to say for himself first. You'd like to take him back at once, I suppose."

"If it is agreeable, yes, but I shall be quite satisfied if he is undair detention," said Monnet. His eyes were very bright; obviously he was delighted with his reception.

"Soon as I saw all this stuff I asked the airport police to bring Forrester up, under guard," said Appleby. "He should be here soon."

"That's good," said Gideon.

He could hear his name being spoken from behind him, and glanced round to see the nondescript sergeant looking as if he was willing his superiors to stop talking. The sergeant had the telephone at his ear, and now he covered the mouthpiece quickly and hissed across:

"Excuse me, sir. Superintendent Wragg on the line. He says it's urgent. Can you—"

"Coming," said Gideon, and heaved himself to his

feet. "'Scuse me." He lumbered across the office, a little stiffly, for something had given him a cramp in his right leg, while the sergeant held the telephone out almost anxiously. In the back of Gideon's mind there were all the things he had learned from Monnet, and the probability that Forrester had in fact killed the girl and buried her body under the rocks in the Pyrenees, doubtless expecting it to stay there for years. The severe winter of the previous year had uncovered the body, for ice and snow had caused a small avalanche, and first a skull had been found, then all the bones and the odds and ends of the girl's belongings which the French police had painstakingly collected and pieced together. Forrester had probably thought his year-old crime almost forgotten.

Now Wragg.

Wragg of GH Division had not sent in any special reports after that of the second baby. He was a self-sufficient type, and if he made a mistake it would be from taking too much upon himself rather than trying to shift responsibility; no time waster, either.

"Gideon," said Gideon into the mouthpiece.

"Thought you'd want to know this," said Wragg. "We've cornered the Prowler."

It was certainly going to be a night to remember.

Gideon put down the receiver, three minutes after he'd had the news, and grinned broadly. Monnet was staring from the other side of the room as Gideon rubbed his great hands together. Sometimes it all went wrong and occasionally—not very often—everything went right, and this was the night of nights. Wragg was sure the cornered man was the Prowler. He had been seen leaving a tube station in Wragg's Division, and Wragg had been extremely thorough; he had not taken

167

all his men away after the official finish of the great hunt. At the approach to all the stations, main bus stops and bridges in the Division, he had slapped white paint, thinned down so that it wouldn't dry quickly, and his men had studied the ' footprints of every passenger.

One of the uniformed men had seen a heel print identical to that which he'd seen on a telephotograph.

"Our chap showed his hand a bit too early, and the Prowler realized what was on," Wragg had said, "so they had a game of hide-and-seek up and down the station. Then the Prowler reached the street, but we had half a dozen men there by then. He got into a little park near the station, and hasn't come out, but I thought you'd like to be at the finish."

"You get him; I'll come if I can," Gideon had said, and then rung off, still grinning and rubbing his hand's together. "Looks as if the Prowler's in the bag, Charley," he added. "How about that?"

Appleby gaped. *"No!"*

"Wragg says yes."

"Must be personal magnetism," said Appleby. "You want 'em and they come. Perhaps I mean hypnotism. Look at the only known policeman who can mesmerize crooks, M. Monnet." Monnet, realizing that there was a cause for rejoicing, rejoiced with them with bright smiles. "Forrester's here in the waiting room," Appleby went on. "I said you'd be right down."

Gideon said more slowly, "Yes, I will." He hesitated, while Monnet watched with obvious anxiety, hoping that he was to be present. Going down to interview a frightened man wanted for inquiries about a year-old murder was a kind of anticlimax, and Gideon would much rather be on his way to see Wragg, but if ever there was a case for *entente cordiale* this was it. "M. Monnet, if you'd like to come down with me you can

168

see and listen to everything from outside the room while I talk to Forrester. Would you?"

"If you *please!*"

"Let's go," said Gideon.

It wasn't going to take long.

Guilt was a thing which you couldn't take for granted, no matter how tempted, and it revealed itself in a variety of odd ways. Sometimes it was so apparent that it seemed too good—for a policeman—to be true. That was the case with Forrester. He was a man in the early thirties, well set up, well dressed in light gray. A diamond tiepin flashed in his tie; his hair was immaculate; if he could have kept his nerve he would have created a very good impression. As it was, he paced the floor of the small waiting room with the window through which no one could see, but through which watchers could see in. As Gideon entered, he spun round, snatching a half-smoked cigarette from his lips.

"Look here, what the hell is all this? Who are you? Why am I being held here? I demand my rights, do you hear? I demand my rights."

"And you shall have them," said Gideon, very quietly. "Don't worry about that, Mr. Forrester." Nine times out of ten the gambit he decided to use would fail, seven times out of ten it would be folly; but he had seldom felt more convinced that it would come off. His tone had silenced Forrester, and he went on quite casually. "What did you do with the money, the diamond ring and brooch which you stole from Miss Guthrie before you killed her?"

Forrester nearly broke down, but something stiffened his resolve and he spoke evenly enough. "I didn't kill her. I don't know anything about it."

169

"Why not tell us the truth? We shall find it out in the long run," Gideon insisted. "Where—"

"I know nothing about it," Forrester declared, his eyes glittering. "I want to see my solicitor, at once—that's if you won't let me go."

"I'm afraid it will take a few days. M. Monnet," Gideon said soon afterward. "I hope you can stay in London; we'll be happy to have you spend some time with us. Of course we'll get everything done as soon as we can, but unless we can break down Forrester's denials—"

"There is no urgent reason for my return," said Monnet, "but I do not want to go back without him."

"We'll break him down if we can," Gideon promised. "I'll detail a Chief Inspector to work with you; just the man to wear Forrester down."

Monnet was grateful, and Gideon took him along to a C.I. whose French was almost as good as Appleby's. Then Gideon went back to his office. Appleby would already know the result of the interview, and he ought to know also whether Wragg had yet caught the Prowler. But Appleby was sitting at the desk writing, no longer showing any sign of excitement. It was nearly four o'clock, and he looked tired.

"He's tough, then?"

"Yes. Anything from—" Gideon hesitated, and then added abruptly: "Hemmingway?"

"No."

"Couldn't slip up there, could he?" asked Gideon musingly, and found himself stifling a yawn. Appleby didn't volunteer anything about the Prowler, which meant that there wasn't any fresh news. It was hardly worth going to see Wragg now, though; inviting being met by a smug superintendent and a handcuffed prisoner. The Office, still warm, was untidy, indicating the amount of work which had been handled in the past eight hours. Long shifts, these night shifts. The sergeant in brown who didn't register was not in the office, but the Divisional reports, with all of Appleby's notes and comments, were on Gideon's desk. He went to it, then realized that he was very hungry; he hadn't had anything at all since a meal with Kate at about five o'clock, except a couple of stiff whiskies.

He sat down, rather heavily.

"Thought you'd go have a bite," said Appleby. "No use neglecting the inner man, Chief."

"Just thinking of that, too, but I think I'll send for a sandwich."

"Two minds," said Appleby, grinning. "I ordered ham *and* beef, tea *and* coffee." He waved a hand at Gideon's smile of appreciation. "You know your trouble, George, don't you?" It was the first time he had brought himself to say "George" and even then it was obviously an effort, for he paused for a moment before adding. "You *work* too hard. Know what they say about all work and no play? Digs a copper's grave next day. I don't know what ticks with people with a metabolism like yours, I don't really."

The door opened and a uniformed man came in from the canteen with sandwiches, tea, coffee, mustard and some cakes coated with sugar icing.

"Thanks," said Gideon. "Fine."

He munched and drank as he looked through the reports. As he knew well from past experience, this was the night's quiet time. If it followed custom, the telephone calls would become more and more infrequent, the sound of Squad cars returning from their different assignments would be clear outside, and soon the day would begin for the rest of London. The charwomen, the men on the way to stoke boilers banked up for the night, the workmen due to start as soon as daylight came would be on the move. As much work as

171

possible would be done on the roads and on electricity, gas and water mains before the throngs began to descend upon the streets. Soon the first buses would approach Parliament Square from each direction, and all the tube lines would be busy again.

Most of the night's crimes had been committed.

Not all, thought Gideon, as he flipped the pages over. In the city or a suburb men might still be drilling the safe of a bank or warehouse, men might be loading lorries at this moment with stolen goods, crooks might have done their job and be sitting in comfort at the scene of it, perhaps having a meal, so that they need not leave too early and so furtively. Any man wandering abroad between one o'clock and half past four was likely to be questioned by the police; after that, the police were likely to assume that he was about his normal business.

So it was not all done.

There was still no word from Wragg, and that worried him; none from Hemmingway or Lemaitre, and that puzzled him. There were other jobs that he knew little about, some that he knew nothing about—one, although he did not realize it, under his very hand.

This was the report from AB Division, and the note about Mrs. Penn and her anxious mother. It was near the bottom of the pile, because it had come in near the end, and Appleby was as methodical as an automat. Gideon glanced across at him and saw, now that the night was well advanced, that Appleby looked tired and old, with deep lines at his forehead and his eyes , others at his lips. All the brightness and the vitality seemed to have been drained out of him, but he sat working doggedly, sifting papers, jotting down notes, suggesting which crook might have committed this job or that, assigning men to inquiries, deciding which case could be left to the Division and which one needed urgent following up by the Yard.

It was very quiet in the office.

Gideon turned a report over, and saw the AB form, typewritten, ran his eye down the first page, which carried a brief and concise report of the baby kidnapping, and two reports of shops being burgled. On the next page was the report from Mrs. Penn's mother. Gideon started to turn the page, seeing Appleby's note on the shop burglaries: *Looks like Pinky White, left-hand job, his usual means of entry: suggest pick him up.*

That would be done in the morning.

Gideon flipped the page.

Sharp and stinging, the telephone rang. It was the first time tonight that it had surprised him, and he glanced up. Appleby had been shaken out of his mechanical movement of hand and pen, too.

"Gideon."

"Mr. Wragg for you, sir."

"Put him through."

"Right away, sir. . . . Here's Mr. Gideon."

"What's on?" asked Gideon, in a voice which betrayed his fear of bad news.

"I hope there's a special bit of brimstone for the Prowler," Wragg said, and Gideon thought with a sudden weight of depression that the man had got away. Then: "Climbed up to a top-floor room of a house overlooking the park. There's a girl in the room. Says he'll kill her if we don't let him go. Sounds as if he'd do it, too," said Wragg, who in turn sounded the most depressed officer in the Force.

15

The Desperate Men

Less than half an hour earlier, Marjorie Hayling had stirred in her sleep, in her one-room flatlet at the top of an old house in a cul-de-sac in Earl's Court. Stirring, she had shifted the bedclothes, uncovering her white shoulder and a little of her arm. A street lamp just outside the house threw a shadow into the room—the shadow of a man who was climbing in. It appeared on the ceiling and then, as he drew further in, on the top of the wall, a dark, moving shadow.

There were sounds outside, footsteps, men calling out, someone saying clearly:

"There he is!"

Another light, that from a powerful torch, had touched the man's feet as he had hauled himself into the room. A small cabinet was close to the window, and he kicked against it and sent it rocking.

That woke the girl.

At first, all she knew was the fear of a fast-beating heart and quick, almost painful breathing, as if she had waked from a nightmare; but gradually the sounds had come into the room. Her eyes had focused on the man coming toward her with his arms outstretched. She could only just make out his hands and his face, although he was so near.

She tried to scream, and he pounced.

She felt his icy fingers at her neck, and struck at him, but her arm caught in the sheet and she could do nothing more to help herself. She saw the glitter in his eyes, then felt the choking pressure at her throat. Suddenly there was a tightness at her lungs, becoming worse and worse until it seemed as if her chest would burst.

Then she lost consciousness.

The Prowler felt her go limp, held on tightly for a moment, then let her fall. For a fleeting moment his hand touched her hair, and there was strange gentleness in the movement, but he heard more sounds below, as of a car drawing up, and he turned to the window, which was still wide open. He stared down, desperately. Fifty feet below were a dozen men, half of them policemen in uniform, most of them staring up. One man held a torch, two pointed, someone exclaimed:

"There he is!"

Another called in a deep, carrying voice. "Don't give us any more trouble; you can't get away."

"If you don't get away from there and let me go I'll kill her!" the Prowler shouted, and his voice was shrill and clear. *"That's what I'll do, I'll kill her."*

A man said, as if shocked, "There's a woman up there."

"I'll kill her!" the Prowler screeched, and then backed from the window and slammed it down so that the walls of the room shook. He darted across the room and switched on the light. The girl lay limp on the bed, her dark hair against the white pillow, bare arms and bare shoulders all uncovered now. He opened the door into the "hall," then the door leading to the landing,

176

and, as he did so, heard a banging; that would be the police trying to get in at the street door. He spun round—all his movements were swift and darting—went into the bedroom and pushed an armchair on squeaking casters toward the landing door. It banged against the wooden panels. He turned the chair on end, then slammed the room door on it. He could feel the pressure; the chair was between the two doors, and he had barricaded himself in better even than he had planned.

He was breathing very hard as he turned round, went to the bed, tore a sheet into strips and bound the girl's hands together tightly.

The noises from the street were muted now, but he crept close to the window and looked out. More cars were on the street, and suddenly a much brighter light shone upward, making him dodge to one side. No one was attempting to climb up the side of the house, and he turned and studied the unconscious girl.

She was breathing very evenly.

He watched her, his eyes narrowing.

He was a slightly built man probably in the middle thirties, with fair, receding hair, a little, pointed nose and rather thin lips. Not bad looking in a way; an ineffectual type if one judged by appearances, the nine-to-six kind of office worker, except that the cut and quality of his clothes were very good. His hands were very large in proportion to his body, and his fingers looked very strong.

He glanced about the room.

In one corner was a small gas stove, and above it some shelves, curtained off, probably containing pots and pans. Near this was a small larder, on a table. The whole of this corner could be curtained off, too, leaving the bed-sitting-room looking fresh and pleasant. It had been recently painted and papered, and the carpet, a patterned green, was new looking. On the small dressing table in the corner there stood a vase of carnations—six pink blooms. The whole room had the look of one who was house-proud.

A small wardrobe stood against one wall.

The man moved to it, and began to shift the wardrobe, gradually pushing it until it was wedged against the door. Now the only possible way in was through the window, and the Prowler seemed to relax when he realized that.

He went to the side of the bed, and touched the girl's hair.

Then a booming voice sounded, almost as if it were in the room, and he made a darting move toward the window.

"Listen, you there! If you open the door and come down, we'll give you a fair deal. We won't hurt you."

He ran his hand across his forehead, and moistened his lips. Then he went close to the window, but he couldn't see out properly so he opened the window a few inches. He was able to see much better. Five cars were in the cul-de-sac, now, and a man stood by one of them with a microphone to his mouth. The voice came again, loud and clear.

"We won't hurt you. Open the door and come out."

He leaned down and put his face close to the opening of the window, and called:

"If you don't let me go I'll kill her!"

"Don't be a fool, you'll only make it worse for yourself."

"I've told you what I'll do. I'll kill her!" the Prowler screeched, and then he slammed the window down.

Marjorie Hayling's eyes were wide open.

She had heard every word.

It was half past four.

A few miles away, across London, Rikker stood by the wall in the passage leading to the cellar of his little house. It was cold, yet he was sweating. His hair, face, shoulders, hands, clothes, everything was covered with a thick film of dust. By his side were a small crowbar, a hammer, a cold chisel and several other tools. Heaps of powder from the cement and the bricks lay on the floor, and the air was filled with the writhing dust.

He kept coughing.

A dozen or so bricks, some broken, some whole, were on the floor just behind him. Chippings of bricks lay about, and now and again, as he moved, he crunched some under his feet. He kept wiping the sweat off his forehead, and his face was streaked with damp grime; there was a crust of dirt on his short, stubby eyelashes.

Suddenly he flung a crowbar down. It clattered noisily as he strode toward the steps which led upward. He had to pass the door which led into the main part of the cellar, where the woman was, and he looked inside.

There she sat, under the light, and he could not tell whether she was awake or unconscious; whether she was alive or dead.

She was still alive, but barely conscious.

Rikker went upstairs. His wife sat in an old saddle back chair, her head back, mouth open, uncanny white teeth showing. She whistled and squeaked as she breathed, her eyes were tightly closed, and he knew that she wasn't pretending sleep. He made as if to wake her, but some whim changed his mind, and he went through into the scullery and washed his hands and doused his face in cold water. He dabbed himself dry, and returned to the kitchen; the running water and the sound of his movements hadn't disturbed his wife. Rikker opened the doors of a cupboard, took out a bottle nearly full of whisky, splashed some into a thick glass, and went into the scullery and filled the glass with water. Then he drank deeply.

Going back, he kicked accidentally against the door, and it slammed. His wife started, her eyes flickered, and she struggled more upright, her lips working as if she was as thirsty as Rikker himself, or else caught by sudden fear.

Her eyes were strangely round and brilliant.

"You done it?" she asked in a gasping voice. "Have you?"

"Lot of use you are," Rikker sneered. "I thought I told you to bring me a drink an hour ago."

She started to struggle to her feet.

"I'll get it, I'll get it!"

"Siddown. I helped meself."

She was quite upright now, staring at him almost as if in horror.

"You—you done it?"

"No."

"I—I thought—" She glanced at a little alarm clock on the mantelpiece. "It's half past four! You said you'd be finished by three, you said—"

"Well, I ain't finished yet," Rikker said roughly.

"W—w—why?"

"The wall's like concrete, and I can't make the hole big enough. Can't make too much noise, can I?"

"How—how much longer will it take you?"

"How the hell do I know?" Rikker demanded. "All I know is I've been working all night, and I'm tired out, see?"

"Can—can I do anything?"

Rikker leered at her.

180

"You can have forty winks while I do the work," he said roughly. He picked up the glass and drank as if the contents were beer, not whisky. He looked tired, and the dust, now caked on his face and especially round his eyes, made it appear as if he had a mask on. "Yeh, you can come and help; I've got more bricks nearly loose now."

She got up eagerly.

"Got to get it finished quick," Rikker went on, almost to himself. "Got to get her inside and the wall patched up again, but—"

"What are you going to do if you can't—*can't* get it finished tonight?"

Rikker growled, "I'm thinking, ain't I?"

He nodded abruptly and then went downstairs, walking very slowly and carefully, so as to make no noise. It was the noise which drove him almost to desperation. He picked up the crowbar, and then his big, heavy boots crunched on the brick chippings. As he prised at some of the bricks he had laid bare, they moved much more easily than they had a few minutes ago, and his shoulders seemed to brace themselves and he worked with great eagerness. His wife picked up a screwdriver and prised more bricks away, and she was able to work almost as quickly as he.

"Looks as if the worst is over," she said. "They're movin' easier."

"Could be." Rikker began to chip at the cement between the bricks, and this was something which took more time and which really needed much more force; but too much force would make a noise which would be heard by the people next door, and that was the one thing which Rikker was desperately anxious not to do.

Then, cement began to crumble.

"Got another soft patch," he said, and there was a glitter in his eyes and he began to work more quickly.

The piles of bricks grew, and the hole in the wall grew. It was a sturdily built cavity wall, as he knew from grim experience.

"Nearly got room already," Mrs. Rikker wheezed, and the dust which had now gathered on her eyes made them shine like polished glass. "How much *more* room do you want?"

"Not much. But I want a rest from this. I'll go and mix the plaster now," said Rikker. "There's plenty left over from last time. You start tidying up, and use plenty of water, or that dust'll be the death of me."

He went into the large cellar. His victim raised her head very slowly, and looked at him with dulled, pained eyes. He scowled and averted his gaze, and went hurriedly toward the corner where there was a small bag of cement and a heap of sand. He shoveled some sand onto a plaster board, picked up the cement and a hand trowel, and began to work.

His wife was coming downstairs with a broom and a bucket of water.

"Get a move on," he called. "This job's giving me the creeps."

At half past four, Tony Melcrino got up from the table, where he had been sitting for so long that his legs ached, and looked down at his Lollo. She was lying back in the armchair, her legs up on a smaller chair, and his thick, belted overcoat round her shoulders. There was no way in which Lollo could look anything but beautiful, not even like this.

She was breathing softly, her lips pouting and quivering, pouting and quivering.

He beckoned several of his boys; they walked across the dance floor, their footsteps echoing. The music had been stopped for a couple of hours, and the members of his gang were sitting round the walls, many of them asleep, a few playing cards. The giggly girl at the bar was lying behind the counter with one of her two boy friends, both fast asleep. The garish room and the dingy festoons and decorations looked even worse. So did the sign that hung so low that it almost touched Melcrino's head.

Youth for Christ Crusade.

Melcrino didn't look his twenty-two years, and might easily have been taken for eighteen or nineteen, partly because he was so small.

Two guards were at the front door.

"See any cops?" Melcrino asked.

"They're quiet."

"Sure they ain't gone?"

"They're around."

"Spike still at the corner?"

"Yeh."

"With Widey's boys?"

"Yeh."

"'Kay. Bert—" Melcrino turned to one of the men who had come from the dance hall with him. "—go and tell Widey I want to talk to him."

"Sure, okay, Melky."

"What are you waiting for?"

"Okay, Melky!" Bert hurried out, and then ran toward the other clubhouse, which was so near and yet was often out of bounds, for the two gangs seldom mixed. Two or three of the Wide boys watched as Bert approached, and word was sent back to Jacky Wide, who was not only leader of the gang but had given it its name.

Bert sent a cryptic message, and the answer came promptly:

"Sure, Melky can come."

"He didn't say he'd come here, he said—"

"Widey'll talk to him but he won't come and lick his shoes," a Wide boy said. "You go and tell Melky that. If he wants to talk, okay, he can come."

Melky was still in the doorway when he got the message. Obviously he didn't like it; as obviously, it didn't surprise him. He put his hand just inside his trousers waistband, where he kept a knife with a sheath which was kept well greased to facilitate quick movement.

"You ain't going to let Widey tell you what you're going to do," Bert protested roughly. "You'd be crazy."

"So the mountain won't come to Mahomet, so what does Mahomet do?" asked Melky, and gave a little grin which many people had learned to dislike. "Two of you come with me." He stepped into the dark street, looked right and left, and then walked quickly toward the Red Lion Gymnasium. The guards at the door let him in without question. He and his two bodyguards were led across the dance floor in this club to something he hadn't got himself—a comfortable living room with easy chairs, a television set and a cocktail cabinet.

Widey had two men with him, small, thickset, very tense looking. Widey himself was taller than most of the members of either gang, not a bad-looking man with a shock of black hair, pale features and a pointed chin; his head was shaped rather like a pear with a very flat top. His eyes were dark blue, and he watched Melky narrowly.

"Want to talk to me, Melky?"

"That's what I said. You know what time it is?"

"Four thirty."

"It's nearly five o'clock," Melky said. "You think that van's coming?"

"It'll come."

"Listen," Melky said, "you wouldn't have had that van stopped before it got here, would you?"

184

Widey looked so startled that his very expression carried conviction. Then he gave a quick grin. He could be very attractive when he grinned; there was a bold air about him, something almost piratical, and a swagger, too.

"That would have been a brain wave, Melky, only I never thought of it!"

"So long as you didn't."

"I didn't," said Widey. "So what's next?"

"Do we still wait?"

"You can go home, but I'm going to wait," said Widey, and his voice became harsher. "We've got the cops drawn off nicely; we don't have anything to worry about. We let the van go through the gate, and then we start the fight, and while the cops are laying for us we take the stuff off the van. That's the way it will be. If you've got cold feet, okay, my boys can fight among themselves. They'll make it look convincing."

"Who said anything about cold feet?"

Widey grinned. "Maybe you have good reason for wanting to go to bed."

"Sometimes I wish I hadn't agreed to string along with you," said Melky, his lips drawn very taut. His right hand was moving close to the favorite spot at his waistband. "Sometimes I think I'll be glad when—"

"Listen, Melky," Widey said, suddenly quite earnest, "if the cops think we're going to war they'll sit back and let us fight it out, see? They'll expect us to cut ourselves up. So that's what we let them think. But you and me, we're too fly for that. A few of the boys are nabbed and maybe they'll get six months, so what do we do? We look after them when they come out, no one's any the worse off. The cops think we're going to sit back and lick our wounds, and that's how much they know, the flickin' so-and-sos. We'll have it all our own way for weeks before they get round to realizing that we ain't dead yet, and then we'll have a rest, see, and they won't be able to pin anything on us. That's the plan we agreed, Melky, what's the matter with keeping it that way?"

Melky didn't speak.

"But just say the word," said Widey, "and I'll go it on my own. I—"

A sharp ringing sound cut across his words, the ringing of a telephone. The phone was behind him, and he turned round swiftly, leaned forward and grabbed it.

"Who's sat? . . ."

"Whassat? . . ."

"Okay!"

He put down the receiver very slowly and turned to look at Melky, his head on one side, his lips twisted in a grin which told its own story. He didn't speak immediately, but seemed to enjoy keeping Melky on tenterhooks. Then he announced:

"The van's on the way. Okay?"

"Okay," breathed Melky. "It'll be here in ten minutes. *Okay*. No knives, no razors, nothing to do any serious harm, that okay?"

"That's the way we planned it, and that's the way it's going to be," said Widey. "You ever known me go back on my word?" He held out his hand. "Shake on it?"

They shook hands.

"Okay," breathed Melky, and turned and hurried out with Bert and the other member of his gang to start the mock fight. In five minutes the "battle" would be at its height, and in five minutes the Post Office van carrying a small fortune would pass through the gateway of the docks.

When he had gone, Wide grinned broadly and evilly, and very slowly took out a double-edged blade fitted into a handle so that it could cut nastily, but not go dangerously deep. Then he went outside to a big barrel

186

by the door and whipped the cloth off the top. It was full of potatoes. His men came hurrying, each dipping into the barrel and picking out two of three potatoes. They looked like ordinary unpeeled potatoes, but buried in each was a double edged razor blade. Many of the men had ugly, spiked knuckle dusters on their hands already.

"So Melky fell for it," Jacky Wide said. "He fell for it good and hard. After tonight there won't be any Melky gang left."

16

Gideon Moves

Gideon heard Wragg's telephone go down, and replaced his own. As he did so, he stood up slowly, and the button of his coat caught the Divisional report he had been reading, and pushed it to one side. The page above that which reported Mrs. Russell's anxiety about her daughter, Netta Penn, fell slowly, and so hid the paragraph from sight. As he moved again, he knocked the report off the desk and stooped down to pick it up.

"The Prowler's shut himself up with a girl and says he'll kill her if we don't let him go," he said to Appleby, quite flatly.

Appleby said, "Gawd, *no.*"

"I'd better go over," said Gideon.

He didn't go to the door at once, but lit a cigarette and deliberated. Appleby pushed his chair back, his eyes brighter, the look of an aging man vanished for a moment.

In fact Gideon was trying to make up his mind about his own motives for wanting to go to Earl's Court at once. The Prowler was his primary reason for coming on duty tonight, and above everything else was the man he wanted—but was it necessary for him to go in person? He knew all the arguments. When a man barricaded himself in and had a hostage, it could be very ugly, for only desperate men did that. There was nothing to suggest that the Prowler had a gun, but he didn't need a gun to kill that girl. If the police had to lay siege, it could last for a long time, and that would mean real trouble in the morning, with the Home Office involved, big newspaper stories inevitable. If he didn't go, and if Wragg didn't get the Prowler while saving the hostage's life, then the Assistant Commissioner, the Commissioner himself and probably the Home Secretary would want to know why the senior official on duty hadn't taken charge.

This wasn't just a question of wanting to finish the job off himself.

"You'd better get over there, quick," said Appleby. "You certainly know how to pick nights, George."

"The Prowler was almost a cert," said Gideon, and he glanced down at the report which he had picked up ready to throw it on the desk. By chance, the page which fell open was the one with the note about Mrs. Russell's report, and he glimpsed the name "Penn."

He read the paragraph quickly.

"What's on now?" asked Appleby.

"That Mrs. Penn," said Gideon. "Remember she rang me, but didn't hold on long enough?"

"Ridgway sent a man round to see her, didn't he?"

"Yes, she wasn't home. Now there's a report from her mother that she wasn't back by two o'clock," said Gideon. "What's worrying me is why she didn't wait to talk to me." He was scowling now. "If she took the trouble to ask for me, why didn't she hold on?"

"Don't ask me."

"It smells," said Gideon. "Charley, have a Squad car

190

go round and see Mrs. Russell now, find out all they can from her and if she's got any idea where her daughter went. Follow it up. Tell the chaps in the car that it's a special from me."

"Gee-up, from Gee-Gee," quipped Appleby.

As he went outside, Gideon shook his head and through his clenched teeth said, "The blurry fool!" and then he began to hurry. The annoyance with Appleby lasted only for a few seconds, and he realized that his own hesitation about what he should do was due to one thing only: he was tired. His eyes were heavy and there was the feel of sandpaper in them, telling its own story. Except for a couple of hours that afternoon he hadn't slept since six o'clock yesterday morning, which meant that he'd been on the go for a straight twenty-four, and he wasn't used to it. Give him three or four such stretches in a row, and there would be nothing to worry about.

It seemed brighter out in the courtyard, and the stars were pale, but it was false dawn. Half past five. Gideon caught a glimpse of a bus passing on Parliament Street, its passenger lights very bright and glittering. Six or seven cars were waiting now, and one of them was beginning to move. Had Appleby been as quick as that, or was it another job? Gideon got into his own car and pulled out, and the squad car drew level.

"You going to Mrs. Russell, at Fulham?"

"Yessir."

"Quick work, keep it up."

Gideon saw the driver's fleeting smile of satisfaction, and let him draw ahead; seconds weren't likely to make any difference at Earl's Court. Why the hell had they let the Prowler get away, anyhow? It was all very well to slap a copper on the back for being observant, but of all the men to let through their fingers!—a brute who had proved only tonight that he would rather kill than be captured.

That reminded Gideon of another job he'd meant to do. He flicked on the radio, and as soon as he was answered he asked:

"How's the Lewis girl out at Brixton?"

"Last we heard, no change," Whittaker told him from Information, "and with that kind of injury if they can hold on for a few hours it often works out all right."

"Yes, good thanks."

"Pleasure. Going out to Wragg?"

"Yes."

"There's a man who's kicking himself," said Whittaker. "Don't tear him all to pieces."

"I'll leave a bit whole," said Gideon, and rang off.

Talking to Whittaker reminded him again of Matthew, and the boy waiting for him outside the garage, the only place where he could rely on having a word with him without his mother knowing. Bad thing to let him think that one parent might take sides without the knowledge of the other, but it had showed him more clearly than he'd ever seen before how little time he really spent with his family, except the Sunday "jam" sessions. He smiled. When he called them "jam" sessions, Pru immediately flew off the handle. To her, music was something almost sacred; her violin was a kind of altar. The thoughts flickered through his mind as he drove fast through the streets, which were gradually coming to life; the occasional bus, the occasional cyclist, here and there a private car. Probably he was passing men with their loot in their pockets, men who wouldn't get picked up for tonight's job, but sooner or later would end up in court.

He'd have a hell of a lot to do when he got back to the office, preparing reports for the men who would take over. The Golightly woman would have to go before the beak; she would have an eight day remand, or course. Forrester would have to be tackled. The four Hatton Gardens men would be up at Bow Street; the hundred and one—

He heard a fire engine roaring, and it rang its bell, apparently for his benefit, clattered past him and then swung round a corner and went the way he was going. It soon disappeared from sight, although he was doing fifty. When he reached Earl's Court, he saw a crowd already gathering, and a policeman obviously on the lookout for him.

"It's a little complicated to find the place, sir, but you turn right here, and then—"

"Get in, and guide me."

"Yes, sir!"

"Anything developed?" Gideon asked as the man sat down, and he knew that this constable, like most who knew him only as a name, was surprised that he talked like a human being.

"Nothing new as far as I know, sir, but I haven't been at the scene myself."

"Hmm. See that fire engine?"

"Mr. Wragg sent for it, sir."

"Ah," said Gideon.

The route was complicated all right, but the journey only took a few minutes. He pulled up near the cul-de-sac. On the other side was a small park, with a single lamp burning in the middle of it. Two policemen were on duty there. Then Gideon reached a corner, with the constable by his side, and saw at least twenty men, six cars and the fire engine; the firemen were already running the turntable up toward the window of a house, but it didn't seem to be the house where the Prowler had been trapped. Wragg was on the lookout, and came hurrying, tall and supple and fresh looking although he'd been on duty just as long as Gideon; that was the difference ten years made.

Yet Gideon was desperately anxious.

"Anything new?"

"No, been waiting for you."

"See any more of him?"

"We use the blower every two or three minutes and tell him we won't hurt him if he comes down, but that's all. We've got men upstairs outside the girl's flatlet, but I don't want to force a way in that way. There are two doors and the Prowler's almost certainly got them both locked. While we were getting both doors down he could strangle her."

"Hmm," said Gideon. "What do you propose to do?"

"I think we ought to try to get in from the roof," said Wragg, and pointed. "That's the house—one with the white paint." Two mobile searchlights had been rigged up, and were shining toward the window from which the Prowler had shouted. "See the way the eaves hang? If we could get a nimble chap up there, with someone to hold onto his feet, he could hang over the edge upside down, and see inside. If he had tear gas—I've sent for some bombs and masks—he could fill the room with the stuff, and give time for the fire escape and some ladders to be run up to the window."

That was all sound enough.

"He might hear the noise on the roof," Gideon objected.

"We've got to take some chance," argued Wragg. "If you ask me, he won't let himself be captured if he can help it. Behaves as if he knows he's finished, and he might as well make it worth while. We can get up to the roof from the back. I've already had some ladders rigged up. Care to see?"

"Yes. If we go straight ahead with the fire escape turntable, you think he'll realize it in time to do more damage?"

"Sure he will," said Wragg. "Look at the position of

194

that window. He can see nearly everything that's going on, and with a man on top of a swaying turntable, you can't judge the position to the inch *quickly*. Once we reach that window, it's got to be quick."

"Yes," Gideon agreed again.

As he spoke, the man who used the blower called out again, and down here his voice was deep and almost too vibrant. There was no response this time, and no sign of movement at the window. Wragg had given orders, and ladders were being placed near the wall, so close that they couldn't be seen unless the Prowler leaned right out. Once the police gained a few minutes to work in, the ladders would be run up to the window and the turntable moved into position.

"Let's go round the back," said Gideon.

Wragg led the way, and a man brought him two tear-gas pistols, rather larger than army revolvers but much lighter. Just round the corner there was a narrow service alley, with a cement path which led to a small back garden of the house. Police were in strength here, too, and neighbors were watching from lighted windows and back doors.

"All for one man," Wragg said, almost bitterly. "Twenty or thirty to one, and we still can't be sure of stopping him doing any harm. I'll have the pants off Cobley, the copper who—"

"Probably feels a damned sight worse than you do," said Gideon. "Tell me about the girl up there."

"All we know is what we got from the people on the ground floor—the owners of the house. They had it turned into one-room flatlets, and let them to business girls. The girl's named Hayling, Marjorie Hayling. Aged twenty-nine. Been here eighteen months. Her boy friend lives a few streets away; we'll probably have him on our rump when he gets to hear of it. The flatlet itself is reached by the top landing. It's a kind of attic room,

195

the only one on that floor. There's a landing door and a tiny hall, bathroom on the right, bed-sitter straight ahead. I've seen a similar entrance downstairs, and the double door makes it the easiest place in the world to barricade. We wouldn't have time to stop the Prowler killing her. I've got the stairs lined with men; if he should try to get out we'll have him," Wragg added. "Trouble is that you can't be sure which way he'll jump. He's crazy."

"He knows what he's doing," Gideon said grimly. "He's frightened."

They reached the back of the house and the ladders which had been run up to the roof. A man in plain clothes was halfway up the ladder, and climbing down. He was a little out of breath when he reached the ground.

"What's it like up there?" asked Wragg.

"Not too bad," the detective officer said. "There's a chimney stack we could fasten a rope round, then we could rope one man to it and he could hold the chap who was going to break the window. Shouldn't cause too much trouble, but it's a long way to fall."

"Have a fire sheet hanging out," said Wragg.

"Tell the Prowler what we're up to," Gideon objected.

There was a pause before Wragg looked toward the service alley, where two men were approaching, one wearing a helmet, one bareheaded; there was sufficient light from the nearby houses to show that obviously he recognized the man, and he scowled.

"That's the copper who let him go. All right, all right, the one who spotted him, too! George—"

"Hmm?"

"We could promise the Prowler that we'd let him go; it might work," said Wragg. "We could withdraw the nearby men, and have the whole area sealed off."

"Yes," agreed Gideon ponderously, "we could. But we couldn't be sure that he wouldn't kill the girl before he left. I know we can't be sure she's alive either, but—" He broke off as the two newcomers drew up, the constable drawing himself rigidly to attention. He was obviously a youngster, and one of those who had barely scraped into the Force by the five feet eight inches height regulation. The light was just good enough to show his tension.

Wragg said to the plain clothes man with him. "Well?"

"Cobley would like to speak to you, sir."

"He's got a tongue, hasn't he?" Wragg said nastily. "What is it?"

Bad, thought Gideon, very bad. It wasn't until they had authority that the best and the worst came out in a man, and for Wragg to talk to anyone like this in front of the others, especially in front of the Commander, was a clear indication that he had a lot to learn about handling men. Pity. This could so easily break this Cobley.

Cobley said abruptly:

"I would like to volunteer for the roof job, sir. I've had training in the army. I'm sure I could do it."

Wragg stared.

Gideon felt helpless. He wanted to whisper. "Don't turn him down, Wragg, don't kill everything he's got." The silence seemed to drag unbearably, but in fact it wasn't yet ten minutes since Gideon had arrived, not more than three since the report had come from the roof.

"What boots you wearing?" asked Wragg abruptly. Ah!

"Regulation, sir, but I could take them off."

"All right," said Wragg. He wasn't gracious, but that didn't matter; obviously he'd seen the folly of smacking

Cobley down too hard. "Where's that tear-gas bomb?"
Another plain-clothes man handed it to him. "You say
you've used these, Cobley."

"Yes, sir, during my army training."

"Do you know what we want to do?"

"Break the window and fill the room with gas before
he can do any harm to the girl, and give the others time
to get in."

"That's right," said Wragg. "If you make a noise on
the roof, or do anything wrong, you might make him
turn on her. And if you fall you'll break your neck."

"I think I can do it, sir."

"Right," said Wragg and turned to Gideon. "I'm
going up to hold his legs. Feel like coming?" He didn't
add that he thought Gideon was too heavy for the roof,
just looked as if he hoped that Gideon would realize it
himself.

"No," said Gideon. "I'm going round to the front and
I'm going to talk to the Prowler while the ladders are
put ready and you're on the go. Good luck, Cobley."

"Thank you, sir," Cobley was still very taut.

Gideon hurried round to the cul-de-sac.

In that room the Prowler was standing by the
window, now peering out, now turning round to look
at Marjorie Hayling. She was sitting bolt upright, and
the fluffy jacket was loose round her shoulders. There
were red, puffy marks at her throat. Several bruises
were already discoloring, and her eyes still held the
brightness of her tears, but she had won control of
herself, and talked rationally and quietly to him.

A different voice boomed over the blower.

"Hello, Prowler! This is Gideon of New Scotland
Yard. I want to talk to you. Open the window."

The Prowler didn't move.

198

"I want to talk to you; open the window," Gideon called. His voice was deeper than that of the first speaker, but it wasn't so vibrant.

The Prowler flattened himself against the wall as he looked down into the street, at the strangely distorted-looking people there, the cars, the fire escape with the turntable some distance from the window. He could not see close to the wall below, could not see the ladders being carried stealthily, almost flush with the wall. His hands were raised in front of him, the fingers clenching and unclenching.

"Open the window; I want to talk to you," came the deep voice.

"Why—don't you see what he has to say?" the girl asked huskily. "He can't hurt you from down there. Why don't you open the window and speak to him?"

The Prowler did not move or answer, but his eyes swiveled round toward her.

"We've got all the time in the world," Gideon called. "Just open the window so that we can talk."

"Why don't you?" the girl pleaded, and she did not stop even when the Prowler glared at her. "I don't know what you've done, but I'm sure they won't hurt you. You'd be wise to give yourself up."

I want to talk to you.

"Why don't you—" the girl began.

"Shut up!" the Prowler spat at her, and suddenly he pulled at the window with his fingers, straining and heaving to get it open; and he opened it an inch and put his face close to the opening and called, *"If you don't go away and let me go I'll choke the life out of her!"*

Then he slammed the window, and turned to face the girl, and she knew that he meant exactly what he said. Yet she did not flinch, just moistened her lips and said:

"It won't help you if you hurt me, will it? If you kill me, you won't have any chance at all, and they'll hate you. But if you give yourself up—"

Gideon heard the shrill note of hopeless defiance in the Prowler's voice, and he had a fair idea of what was going on inside the man's head. For a long time he had got used to having everything his own way, and for a long time he had lived with only one fear: of the police. Now all those pentup fears were bursting out and he could not think beyond the burning desire to get away. Fear and tension bore at him. He had preyed on helpless girls for a long, long time, and now one was helpless in that room with him, and the only weapon he could think of was his power over her.

He was used to using such power.

He had used it murderously tonight.

He might again.

Gideon switched off the blower and spoke to a man standing by him, in a quiet voice which hardly carried.

"Tell that chap over there to start his engine."

"Yes, sir."

"Have him drive to the corner, and keep the engine going," said Gideon, "and tell two other drivers to start up, too."

"Right, sir."

The man went off, and a car engine broke the quiet. Now three extending ladders were in position, two men standing by each, ready to run the ladders right up to the window.

Dozens of people were staring up at the window, which was in the spotlight; many on their way to the station paused to look. There was a rumbling sound, of an underground train in the distance. The engines of several cars made more noise than there had been in the cul-de-sac all the time, but it seemed normal enough— as if several of the police cars were going away.

The noise would reach the Prowler, and would muffle any sounds made on the roof.

Then, Gideon saw the head of P.C. Cobley, edging over the guttering: and he saw the way his hands gripped the gutter. Gideon had passed the word that no one was to exclaim or point or draw attention to the roof, for fear the Prowler would notice what they were doing, and he had to guard himself, watching covertly, his heart sick with apprehension.

Cobley was much further over, his head and shoulders showing now. One hand disappeared; then he brought it into view again, holding a bomb. He wriggled forward inch by inch, and it seemed to take an age. The car engines were still warming up, and there was no sign of movement at the window of the room.

Now, Cobley was leaning right over, bent double at the waist. He was just above the window. A little further over, and he would be able to see into the room. Now the light shone on his fair head, and on the bomb, which looked almost black. Gideon could imagine the pain at his thighs as he put all his weight on them.

"For gossake get a move on!" muttered a man by Gideon's side.

He was clenching his hands and gritting his teeth.

17

One Job Over

Everyone in the cul-de-sac was watching tensely, even though there was a risk that the Prowler would realize what was happening. There was no sign of movement inside the room, no shadow, nothing at all. Gideon moved toward the blower again, switched it on, and added to the almost screaming tension by saying quietly.

"You had time to think it over, now, so what about it? We won't hurt you; come out and give yourself up."

Silence.

Cobley edged still further on. He could not control the aim of the bomb yet; he needed another inch or two. The blood must have rushed to his head a long time ago. He might not be able to keep there much longer, might black out. Wragg would be stretched to his limit, too.

"Open the window and talk to me," Gideon called, "Don't be a fool. I might be able to strike a bargain with you."

Silence.

"If you're worried about the girl in Brixton, you

needn't be," said Gideon. "She isn't dead. We want to help you, but we can't if you won't come and listen."

Still silence.

Cobley was edging himself toward his left side now. In a moment or two his head would be below the top of the window, and the important thing was to distract the Prowler's attention. There was no way of being sure that they could; a slight shadowy movement, even a rustle of sound, might be noticed.

Then the Prowler came close to the window.

"Let's be reasonable about it," Gideon said, and he kept his voice quite steady. "Let's talk it over."

He could see the Prowler standing there, as he had a few minutes before when he had opened the window and shouted defiance. Now he hesitated. Cobley was lowering his right hand, and he was also being lowered slowly; it would be only a moment before he could act.

The Prowler opened the window.

"If you don't let me go I'll kill—"

Then there was a swift flurry of movement, the savage thrust of Cobley's fist at the window, the crash of breaking glass. Cobley hurled the bomb as the Prowler backed into the room. Already the ladders were being run up, the fire engine and turntable were on the way; the little street seemed in turmoil as masked men stood ready to hurl themselves at the ladders.

Then a woman screamed.

Cobley was falling.

Two men rushed forward to try to break his fall.

And inside the room there was the cloud of gas, near

204

the window, the girl on the bed, quite helpless.

"No!" she gasped. *"No!"*

She saw the way the Prowler swung toward her, and knew that if he could he would kill her. On he came and she screamed as gas bit at her eyes and nose and throat. He looked crazed as he reached her. She felt the grip of his hands, and did not think that she would ever breathe again.

Then a man came hurtling in at the window.

She felt the Prowler release her, saw him turn round, and saw the other man, blood streaming from a gash in his hand, leap bodily toward him. Other men followed, all masked and grotesque and moving swiftly.

The sharp pain at her eyes and nose was getting worse; she could hardly breathe; but there was no danger from the thin-faced man, no more danger from the Prowler.

"How's Cobley?" asked Gidéon gruffly.

"Broken right leg, cracked ribs, concussion," Wragg said. "It'll keep him away for a month or so! Not much doubt that the Prowler would have killed her if he'd had a little more time. Well, the Prowler won't give the newspapers any more Roman holidays. The Hayling girl will be all right. There was hardly any need to send her to the hospital, but better to play safe." He was talking a little too quickly, almost garrulously. "That's the lot, I think."

Gideon looked down at the papers and oddments which had been taken from the Prowler's pockets, and which a sergeant was examining. He was putting the money and impersonal things to one side and pushing those which looked interesting toward Gideon and Wragg. They were in a downstairs room at the house where the Prowler had taken refuge and the things from his pockets were on the deal-topped table.

The Prowler himself, handcuffed to a detective, was already on his way to the Yard.

He hadn't said a word.

Gideon picked up a crocodile-skin wallet, felt it, looked at it, and said:

"This isn't plastic; it's the real stuff."

"Look at that," said Wragg, and lifted a slim gold cigarette case.

"Monogram on the lighter," Gideon said, and opened the wallet. "Stuffed with notes." A curious kind of tension came back into the room, even when it had looked as if this would be a kind of anti-climax. He took some papers out of the wallet, and read in the same almost startled voice, "The Hon. Alistair Campbell Gore, twenty-nine Moniham Square, W.I. Hear that, Wragg? He's young Campbell-Gore, he—" Gideon's voice cracked.

"What do you know?" said Wragg weakly. "Chap inherits half a million quid one year, and starts going on this kind of prowl the next! It doesn't make any sense."

"It's going to make the biggest noise we've heard for a long time," said Gideon. "I thought I'd seen him before, that pinched little nose and—well, that's it, now I've seen everything. Get it all ship-shape, will you?"

"I will!"

"And let me have reports on Cobley."

"I will. Where you off to?"

"The Yard," said Gideon. "Home from home."

He left the house at once. A small car had just drawn up near the police cars, and he wondered if this was the press. He turned in the other direction and crossed the road without, apparently, being recognized. That way it took him more than two minutes to get to his car, but

206

better that than to stand and talk to the newspapermen; and if he just brushed them off, they wouldn't like it and it wouldn't do anyone any good. His car was far enough from the end of the cul-de-sac not to attract any particular attention, and he got in and drove off. Now a steady stream of people was heading for the tube station, and groups of three or four were waiting at all the bus stops. What time was it? Nearly six. Well, it hadn't taken long, but at one time it had seemed unending. It would be a long time before he forgot the way his heart lurched when Cobley had started his daring leap.

And the Hon. Alistair Campbell-Gore—

"I give up," Gideon said, and then flicked on the radio. They had caught the Prowler, but no reaction of triumph had come with it, and he realized that the tension of the last scenes had added to his tiredness. If he had his way he would put his head down for a couple of hours, and there wasn't a chance. The only big job outstanding was the gang trouble out at the docks, and he was half inclined to believe that it would die a natural death. In spite of the truculence, the gang leaders might have decided that it wasn't worth risking a clash with the police.

"Hello, Charley," he said.

"Strewth, you haven't half missed a birthday party, you have," said Appleby, and his voice seemed to be filled with genuine excitement. "It's still on, too, if you get a move on you ought to see the last act. All the world's a stage, and—"

"Never mind Shakespeare, what's happening?"

"The Melky gang and the Wide boys," said Appleby. "Dunno what went wrong, but something did. Hemmingway fixed the van. When Melky and Jacky Wide opened the doors at the back, half a dozen of our chaps jumped out, and they didn't mind using their truncheons. That was soon over. But the Wide boys were just tearing into Melky's gang. They were about even in number but the Wide boys simply cut them up. That Jacky Wide seems—"

"What else has come in?"

"Only unusual thing's from Willesden. Chap's dug up some human bones in his back garden. I sent Piper over. Nothing urgent."

"I'll go straight to NE Division," said Gideon. "Don't tell 'em I'm coming."

He had to drive past the end of Lassiter Street.

He saw a car standing halfway along it, and two heavily built men standing by the car; that was the Flying Squad, and they didn't seem to be in any great hurry or to have anything much on their minds.

Gideon was half a mile from the two clubs when he saw the first evidences of the fight: two ambulances, coming away from the scene of it. Driving through the little mean streets as a gray light filtered into the sky, he saw more. Here and there a man crept along the pavement by himself, one holding his arm up as if it hurt, another with a bloody head, a third limping. Two police cars, each carrying two of the "boys" and two policemen, passed. Nearer the clubs, there was the noise of shouting and scuffling. At the corner where Gideon had waited earlier, four men were struggling— two "boys" and two plain clothes policemen. Round the corner and nearer the first club were three or four other struggling groups and several men on the ground, but the thing that worried Gideon most was that the police were involved in each of the struggles; there was no question here of the Wide boys fighting Melky's gang. He couldn't drive along this street, so he left the car in the middle of the road and hurried toward the corner, for the worst of the fighting would probably be in the street between the two clubs.

It was not.

There were signs of a fight, though. Battered hats, caps, sticks and, like a litter of paper, little pieces of potatoes, some whole potatoes, and, sparkling in the lights from the street lamps and the clubs, the brightness of steel. He only needed a glance to tell what had happened.

Two policemen were outside each of the clubs, and he asked the same question:

"Mr. Hemmingway here?"

"No, sir."

"No, sir," the second man said, "they—Mr. Hemmingway and Mr. Lemaitre, that is—they went to the docks."

"Right," said Gideon. "Thanks." It was a long walk from the gateway just ahead to the quayside, and he didn't want to tackle it, but there was no car in sight. He walked as briskly as he could toward the gateway, and saw several police cars coming toward him; three in all. He recognized Hemmingway in the first, but not Lemaitre. Hemmingway slowed down; he looked bitter and angry.

"Room for me?" asked Gideon.

"Hop in."

Gideon got in.

"How'd it go?" asked Gideon.

"First time I've ever felt like throwing my hands in," Hemmingway said roughly, and he looked vicious and angry. "This is my beat and I ought to know how their minds tick, but Jacky Wide fooled me." He glanced sideways at Gideon. "He fooled you, too, and he fooled Melcrino. We picked up *one* of the Wide boys—one, out of that mob—and got bits of the story out of him. Widey was after the stuff from the van all right, but it wasn't his first objective; he didn't mind if he let it go. He made a deal with Melcrino to stage a mock fight to fool us, while some of the gang was holding up the van. Melcrino thought he was on the level, and started to fight with the gloves on. Jack Wide didn't. His boys used razors, knives, and knuckle dusters, and the Melky gang didn't have a chance. I don't mind telling you that for once I felt almost sorry for them. We've picked up about twenty of them already, and sent them to the hospital, and there'll be as many being nursed at home. Take it from me, George, the Melky gang doesn't exist any more. The few who didn't get hurt will rat on Melky and go in with Jack Wide. And the *Wide* boys—"

He broke off. This was the thing that really hurt, the thing that Gideon wasn't going to enjoy hearing.

"Well, let's have it."

"The Wide boys had it all laid on. That's the truth. They'd pretty well finished the Melky gang before we weighed in. They knew we were coming, and what did they do? They went through this gateway here like a lot of rats. They'd chosen a night this week because the gates were down. They went straight to the docks, where four old motorboats were tuned up and waiting—pleasure boats being prepared for next summer; the dock police didn't know that the men working on them were Wide boys. They did a darn near perfect job, George—even had two fake warehouse raids up the river that held the River Police while they headed for the Surrey bank. Made it, too. We could see 'em scrambling up on the other side; the tide was pretty high and they didn't have any trouble. They'll all get home without a scratch, and Jacky Wide will be cock o' the walk for a hell of a long time to come—and ask yourself where we'll be?"

"Take it easy," Gideon said quietly, "and get the word put round quickly that the Post Office hold-up job was Wide's idea, and we stopped him and drove him and his boys across the river. That might help a bit."

"Oh, it will help," agreed Hemmingway, "but the truth's the truth, George. Jacky's ten times as strong as he was, and we're going to have a lot of trouble with him in the future."

Of course, he was right. Not only in the Division but in the neighboring Divisions, there would be a time of tension and setbacks. The police would make as big a smoke screen as they liked, but wouldn't be able to hide the truth.

"Any news of Melcrino?" Gideon asked.

"We've got him, and he'll cool his heels for six months or so," said Hemmingway. "Funny thing, though—they didn't touch his Lollo, just told her she wouldn't be hurt, and she could go home to her kids. She went, too. That's what I mean about Jacky Wide," the Divisional man added bitterly. "He's smart, and I *mean* smart. Letting Lollo go free is just the right touch. Wide would put most people against him if he'd hurt her, but now he'll be a kind of whiteheaded boy."

"You'll find a way to black his nose as well as his head," Gideon said.

Then he yawned.

On his way back, along roads which were much thicker with traffic, and where every other vehicle coming toward him seemed to be loaded with vegetables, fruit and flowers from Covent Gardens, he told himself that this was one of the worst setbacks Hemmingway had ever had, and he, Gideon, couldn't escape blame. They hadn't given Jacky Wide enough credit for being smart. A really capable organizer in the

211

East End could be a Divisional and a Yard headache for years. Well, you couldn't have it all ways. When he'd got the Prowler and saved the Hayling girl it had looked as if practically everything had gone right that night; but it seldom worked out that way.

Anyhow, the night was over.

It was turned half past six. The light in the sky was the real dawn, although it took a long time coming, and there was a haze overhead as if the fog was coming back. The wind had dropped. He was glad that driving wasn't difficult, and found himself looking forward with something near repugnance to the task of getting all the reports signed and prepared for the fresh men in the morning—but he would have to make a good job of it. He and Lemaitre usually took over together and, if they had poor or patchy reports from the night-duty men, the air was always blue.

He didn't switch on the radio.

He went by a different route, missing Lassiter Street this time, and driving along Throgmorton Street where the light had been on at the window last night. It would be months, perhaps years, before he had the slightest suspicion of the crime being planned when he had driven past that night.

It was a quarter to seven when he reached the Yard. The atmosphere was quite different now. More cars were about; several of the day men were already in, men who were fresh from their night's rest and walked with enviable briskness. Gideon squared his shoulders and put a spring into his walk, and played with his pipe as he went into the lift with two Chief Inspectors, who wanted to know what kind of a night it had been. He told them about the gang fight, and that the Prowler was now being questioned, then hurried along to his own room and Appleby.

Appleby looked every week of his age now, thin and

gray and pale, but his eyes were still bright and he gave a ready grin as Gideon stepped into the room. By his side was a mammoth pile of reports, and he slapped a hand on them and said:

"All ready and correct, sir, just want your okay. Only one job outstanding as far as I can tell, and I don't mean the NE fiasco or the Prowler."

"What is it?" asked Gideon.

"That Lassiter Street inquiry," said Appleby. "Mrs. Penn called there last night, it seems, and she hasn't been home since. Neighbors say there's been a lot of noise going on. Shall we have a go, or wait until the day staff arrive?"

He looked almost longingly at the clock on the wall.

18

Night's End

Here was the thing which people forgot, Gideon thought tensely as he looked at Appleby: the human factor, the fact that coppers got tired. You could get over physical tiredness, but if you got a touch of mental fatigue it could lead to serious trouble. Probably that was the reason for Hemmingway's failure to grasp the full significance of what was happening in his Division; as likely, it was the reason why he himself was so dispirited. He, George Gideon, had been ready to sleep on his feet when he had walked along the passage, but that feeling had gone, and he knew one thing for certain: mental weariness hadn't yet caught up with him.

He wanted to send Appleby home, he wanted to go to Lassiter Street, and he didn't want to leave anyone else in charge here.

There were footsteps outside, the door opened, and Lemaitre came in briskly. He raised a hand in greeting, took out cigarettes with an almost automatic movement, put one to his lips and said perkily:

"All ready and correct, sir, reporting for duty."

"What's cheered you up?" demanded Gideon.

"Got mixed up with a couple of Melky's boys and proved to myself that I'm still as good as any three of them," said Lemaitre. His eyes had a rather hard, shiny look, but he was fifteen years younger than Appleby, and a night without sleep wouldn't do him any harm. He had been able to work off his despair, too, and probably it wouldn't hit him so hard again in future; when his Fifi had walked out on him, she might have done him a lot of good.

"All right, you take over from Charley," said Gideon promptly. "I'm going to Lassiter Street."

"That Penn business?"

"Yes."

"Ten to one there's nothing to it," said Lemaitre airily. "Ready to go, Charley?"

"Won't take me long to hand over," said Appleby, "but I want to nip along to the end room for a minute." Odd thing, thought Gideon, Appleby could be as coarse and vulgar as any man, but always used the euphemism "end room." Gideon clapped his hat on the back of his head and went to the door, where Appleby joined him quickly, and they walked briskly toward the lift and the head of the stairs. "As a matter of fact," said Appleby, "I just wanted a word in your ear, George."

"Eh? Well, go ahead."

"Until tonight I always had a bellyache about still being a C.I.," said Appleby very slowly. "I always thought you Supers were damn lucky, you most of all, and that I was passed over because of my accent, not lack of ability. This is where I want to say I was wrong. Been a pleasure working with you, George, and I couldn't get anywhere near the standard you set even if I had my time over again."

He was staring straight ahead.

So was Gideon.

They went on for a few paces in silence, and then Gideon said gruffly:

"I've got fifteen years here yet, Charley, if I don't get pushed out earlier, or get knocked over by a bus, and what you've just said is one of the things I'm going to remember as long as I'm here. Thanks." He could have said that Appleby had opened his eyes too, showing unsuspected qualities, but this wasn't the moment; it would look like words for words' sake. There was a much better way, for they reached the lift, and he stopped and said, "Good night, Charley. Like to come on to day duty?"

"Just between you and me, I wouldn't mind," said Appleby. "These jam sessions at night take it out of me."

"I'll fix it," promised Gideon, and then held out his hand. "Good night, Charley."

They gripped.

Then Appleby grinned and turned toward the door marked *Gentlemen,* and said with a waggish air of flippancy:

"Thanks Gee-Gee. Now I'm here, I might as well pop in for a Jimmy Riddle."

Gideon chuckled as he vanished, and as the lift came up. He was still smiling when he reached the Yard. Different men were on duty in the hall, more men were about, a little group of girls on the office staff was coming in, there were charwomen in the passages and in the offices where doors were propped open. He went hurrying to his car, throwing "Morning," "Morning" right and left, and drove out into the brightening day. He had a fairly clear run to Lassiter Street, and on the last five minutes he wondered exactly what "a lot of noise going on" implied. With luck he would soon know. He turned into Lassiter Street and now found two Squad cars waiting, a uniformed man on duty, and

217

a little crowd of early-morning watchers. A milkman was rattling his bottles and a newsboy came cycling along, whistling, and as he drew level with Gideon he shouted:

"Better look out, lot o' coppers along there!"

Gideon drew up behind the cars. The front door of Number 11 was open, and he could see the broad shoulders of a Flying Squad man just inside, and thought he heard a woman's protesting, whining voice. In the distance he heard the ringing of a fire engine or an ambulance. The constable recognized him and stood aside, and he went hurrying.

"I tried to stop him," the woman was saying in a thin, nasal voice. "You can't blame me, I tried to stop him, that's Gawd's truth, everything I could, I did."

Stop *what?*

"What's on?" Gideon asked sharply.

The Squad man turned round. The woman, with her wispy gray hair and thin, dirty face and drab clothes, was cringing back against the wall. There were sounds from below Gideon, and a door below the stairs—the door leading to the cellar—was wide open, and electric light shone out.

"Found the woman—Mrs. Penn, that is—down in the cellar, sir," the Squad man said. "They were going to brick her up in the wall."

"What?"

"You can't blame me, I tried to stop him," the drab whined again. "I did everything I could, I swear I did."

"How long's she been dead?" Gideon asked, and he felt as if he was being choked, for only he could have made sure that more was done here during the night; he should have followed that hunch much earlier.

"Not long," said the Squad man, "no sign of *rigor* yet. Strangled. She was tied to a chair. I'd hang this pair so high—" He broke off abruptly, and then

218

added, "There's the ambulance. I'll go get the men." He hurried past Gideon, while the drab clutched at Gideon's sleeve with skinny fingers, Gideon shook her off, went through the doorway with his head lowered, and went down the flight of stone steps. There were brick chippings, thick dust, the floor roughly wiped over; and there was the hole in the wall and everything that it signified. Two Squad men were in the little passage where the hole had been made, and they were knocking at some bricks a little way further along.

"Found anything else?" Gideon demanded.

"Her husband disappeared, and a hole's been bricked up here," one of the men said ominously.

"Keep at it." Gideon went through into the main cellar, and still had to keep his head low, or he would have touched the ceiling. There lying on the detectives' coats, was the body of a slight, dark, pale-faced young woman whose eyes and mouth were slack; by her side were two silent Yard men. In a corner was a short, stocky, gray-haired man, with a low forehead and a brutal face, a thieves'-kitchen character in real life. Two more Squad men were with him. On the floor near them were a bag of cement, some sand, a pail of water—everything needed to cement the wall.

"Charged him yet?" asked Gideon. He had to speak, to say something.

"No, sir, waiting to see what else we find."

"Right. Who is he?"

"Name of Bartholomew Rikker, sir, owns the house."

"He admitted anything?"

"Won't say a word."

"He will," said Gideon harshly, while Rikker stood there in flat defiance. Then men came hurrying down the stairs, carrying a folded stretcher between them, and it wasn't long before the body of Mrs. Penn was

219

lifted gently onto the stretcher and then carried out. Gideon had one look at her face, and felt a surge of anger which made him clench his hands as he looked at Rikker.

He'd hang him high, too.

He went into the passage.

The men had prised some of the bricks loose. He tried to persuade himself that the girl's husband's disappearance had nothing to do with this bricked-up hole, but at heart he felt sure what they were going to find. It was five minutes before they started the "new" hole. That was all they needed to know; the smell was evidence enough before they found the body.

Rikker refused to say a word, except to demand his "rights"—free legal aid—but his wife didn't take much persuading to talk.

On the night when Michael Penn had come home earlier than his wife, he had been in high spirits and carrying presents for his Netta, and he had told the Rikkers why. He had won nearly two hundred pounds on the weekly pools—for which he always used his office address—and the check had reached him that morning. He had cashed it, spent a little on luxury, and taken the rest home to gladden Netta's heart—one hundred and ninety pounds in one-pound notes.

And the Rikkers had barely enough money to subsist on.

If the woman could be believed, Rikker had wanted to borrow some of the money, Penn had refused and told him that the first thing he would do would be to get out of the two dingy rooms upstairs, and there had been a fierce quarrel.

"I'm sure he didn't mean to kill him. I'm positive he didn't," Mrs. Rikker said drably. "It was really an accident."

"Like the accident to Mrs. Penn," said Gideon.

He didn't say so, and probably wouldn't say so to

220

any but his closest friends, but this was the kind of job which made him curse the names of the Members of Parliament who had fought to put an end to hanging. Hadn't Rikker forfeited all right to live?

The Rikkers were at Cannon Row, and would come up at West London Court later in the morning. The preparing of the charge wouldn't take very long; it was the last thing Gideon would do at the office. He walked across to the Yard building, in broad daylight. He felt as if he had failed utterly, but sheer tiredness overcame depression. He yawned two or three times on the way to his office, and, when he reached it, yawned more widely.

Lemaitre looked up alertly.

"Hello, George, tired?" He leaned back in his chair and tapped the pile of reports which Appleby had left. "Well, you haven't much to worry about. These are all in apple-pie order, hardly any need to do more than initial them." He paused. "Bad show, the Penn murder."

Gideon grunted.

"Don't start blaming yourself. If it hadn't been for you Rikker would have got away with it," Lemaitre said. "The only other thing that went sour on us was the Wide boys' job. There isn't much we need worry about. The Prowler's illustrious ma and pa are downstairs but I wished them onto the secretary's office; no need for us to tackle them yet. The Prowler can thank his lucky stars his wasn't a capital charge, too."

"Jennifer Lewis all right, then?" Gideon was eager.

"Good chance of recovery, according to the hospital."

"Thank the Lord for that," said Gideon. "All right, let me see the reports you think I ought to see."

Lemaitre handed a bunch of reports over, and Gideon was about to go through them when he heard a commotion outside. Then a man began to laugh uproariously. Another joined in. Two more came toward the door, their footsteps almost drowned by the deep-bellied laughter. Lemaitre glanced up, his head on one side, and Gideon said irritably:

"Well, that's one way to start a day."

He expected the men to pass; instead, the door was flung open without warning, and Appleby, wearing his hat and coat and all ready to leave, came striding in, still laughing and looking as happy as if he'd won a fortune. He held his flat stomach until he was able to speak coherently.

". . . never believe it," he said at last. "Greatest joke I've heard in years!" He burst out laughing again, while a C.I. in the passage was grinning broadly, and Gideon clenched his teeth. "You—you know Bigamy Bill had a blonde—"

He couldn't go on. Lemaitre and Gideon exchanged glances as they waited.

"He thought he was on—an easy picking," Appleby went on, his voice husky, "but do you know what she did? She—cor, strike a light! she absolutely cleaned him out! Loose money, watch, cuff links, took everything she could lay her hands on, she did. When he woke at half past six, she wasn't in bed with him, she'd gone."

Lemaitre began to chuckle, and even Gideon grinned.

"Don't tell me B.B.'s reported to us—" Lemaitre said.

"Not on your life; he wouldn't dare show his face. But he kicked up a hell of a fuss, and got his landlady out of bed. Take it from me, *she'll* talk. George, there's a problem, what do we do if he does report it? Do we try to catch the blonde?"

*   *   *

One thing was certain; this had made Appleby's night. He left soon afterward, still grinning and chuckling, and Gideon turned back to the reports, the depression eased. He couldn't fault anything which Appleby had done or recommended and left behind, so he initialed what had to be done, yawned again, stood up, and took his hat and coat off the peg again. Lemaitre, talking on the telephone, looked up and waved, but Gideon didn't go. Lemaitre would probably find the lonely nights the worst time, for a while, and here was the chance to kill two birds with one stone.

Lemaitre finished, and banged down the receiver.

"Copper conked at Camberwell," he said. "No great harm done. Don't you want to go home?"

"Lem, how'd you like to give Appleby a break?"

"Eh? How?"

"He's had all the night work he wants for a bit."

"Oh," said Lemaitre slowly, and looked surprised. He frowned; then his face began to clear and finally he smiled rather tautly, and nodded. "See what you mean. Good idea if I don't have to go home every night. Okay, George, ta."

Gideon nodded and went out. . . .

Soon he was driving homeward, his stream of traffic very thin, the inward stream thick and fast, and a lot of the drivers in too much of a hurry. That was normal. He was checking everything that had happened and trying to make sure that he hadn't forgotten anything significant; certainly there was nothing that couldn't wait. He would spend the rest of the week on night duty, and get back on days next week.

Meanwhile, Kate would be cooking breakfast for the kids, if she hadn't finished already, and it would be good to see her bright eyes and fresh face, her spotless white blouse and—

He slowed down.

At the corner where he turned off the main road, there was young Matthew, leather satchel slung over his shoulders, school cap at the back of his head, obviously waiting for something and not for a bus, for that was further along the road. He recognized the car, and waved eagerly. Gideon hoped that he wasn't going to ask for a lift to school, and a continuation of the discussion of last night. Here he was, round face scrubbed, teeth shining, a little pimply although he seemed to be over the worst of those troubles.

"Morning, Matt."

"Thought I'd catch you," greeted Matthew eagerly, and he leaned against the window but showed no desire to get into the car. "Just wanted a word, Dad. I thought you ought to know. When I got back last night I couldn't help talking about where I'd been, and I thought I might as well strike while the iron was hot, so I told Mum what I'm going to do for a living. She didn't seem to mind as much as I thought she would. Do you know what she said?"

"No, what?"

"She said that she'd be a happy mother if I ever turned out to be half as good a copper as my father! So I told her I'd have a damned—I mean a darned—good try."